When you first meet Nawal, you will be captivated by her smile, her commitment for the people of determination and her keen business sense. She is a force in the accessibility community. Respected by her peers and clients, she has expanded her company, Massiraa, from France to UAE, and now the US. Nawal Benzaouia has had a passion for writing since she held her first crayon, which inspired her to write about her sister with Down syndrome. She became inspired to start writing books because she saw a need for a book that encourages parents, kids, individuals to see beyond each impairment. Behind each disability, there is an ability.

MAYA AND GRACE

THE TALE OF THE GIRL WITH NO HAIR

Nawal Benzaouia

AUSTIN MACAULEY PUBLISHERS™
LONDON • CAMBRIDGE • NEW YORK • SHARJAH

Copyright © Nawal Benzaouia 2023

The right of **Nawal Benzaouia** to be identified as author of this work has been asserted by the author in accordance with Federal Law No. (7) of UAE, Year 2002, Concerning Copyrights and Neighboring Rights.

All rights reserved. No part of this publication may be reproduced, stored in a retrieval system, or transmitted in any form or by any means, electronic, mechanical, photocopying, recording, or otherwise, without the prior permission of the publishers.

Any person who commits any unauthorized act in relation to this publication may be liable to legal prosecution and civil claims for damages.

The age group that matches the content of the books has been classified according to the age classification system issued by the Ministry of Culture and Youth.

ISBN - 9789948808619 - (Paperback)
ISBN - 9789948808626 - (E-book)

Application Number: MC-10-01-6526016
Age Classification: 10-12

First Published 2023
AUSTIN MACAULEY PUBLISHERS FZE
Sharjah Publishing City
P.O Box [519201]
Sharjah, UAE
www.austinmacauley.ae
+971 655 95 202

Acknowledgement

My life is filled with many adventures that I love to write.
Since my childhood, I was going everywhere with a pen and a note book, I have thousands of them full of thoughts, life adventures, and quotes.

To my son, I wish that this book will guide you.
Keep questioning, learning, and discovering. It's a great big world out there—go explore and learn about its ambivalence.

To my family, my sister Sanae who laughed at the first illustration, my sister Salwa who recognized herself and hugged me so tight to thank me. To my brother who will smile while reading the book. To my elder sister and my nephew. To my Father who always bought books for me and to my mother who always pray for me.
My husband who shows me every day that dreams can come true.

And to EVERYONE who ever said anything positive to me or taught me something. I heard it all.

To all children who have ever felt different.

Once upon a time in a far faraway kingdom, there was a girl with no hair called Grace. Grace lived with her sister Maya in an old abandoned castle which was one thousand and one steps from the Mouchi village.

The castle was once known for the great generosity of the Poro family. Every year, the Poro family would hold a big banquet to celebrate the beginning of autumn. This was a special season for the village because the sales of wheat, potatoes and pumpkins were higher.

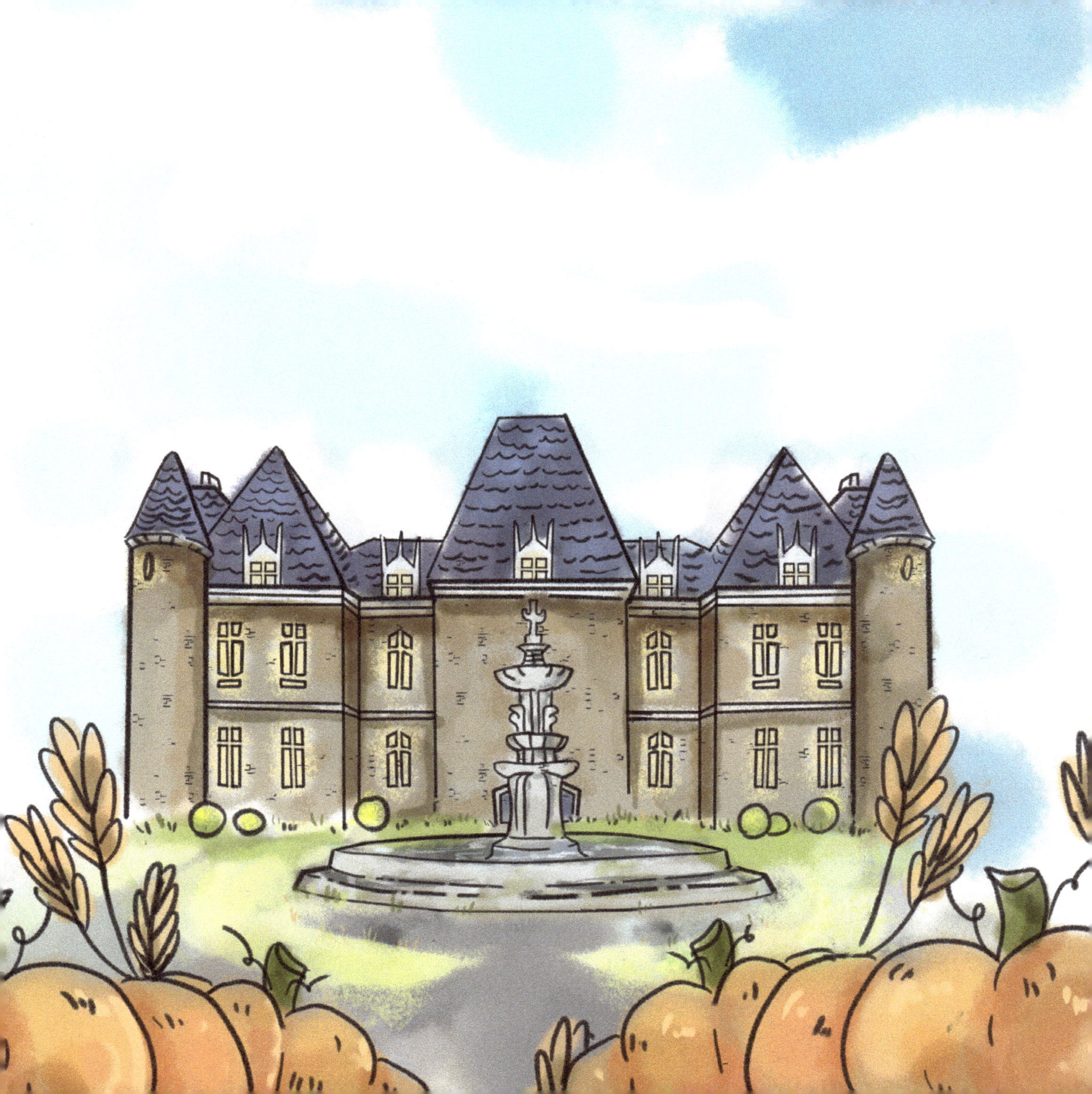

The Poro family was composed of the mother Nadia, Abel the father, three young boys whose recklessness made them stand out and a young girl, Maya whose beauty could rock the moon.

Maya was a bubbly girl full of life. She loved to sing, laugh and smile at the birds outside her window. Maya knew that life was full of mystery and was eager to discover and experience things outside the castle!

Every morning when she opened the window, she imagined what life outside the castle might be like.

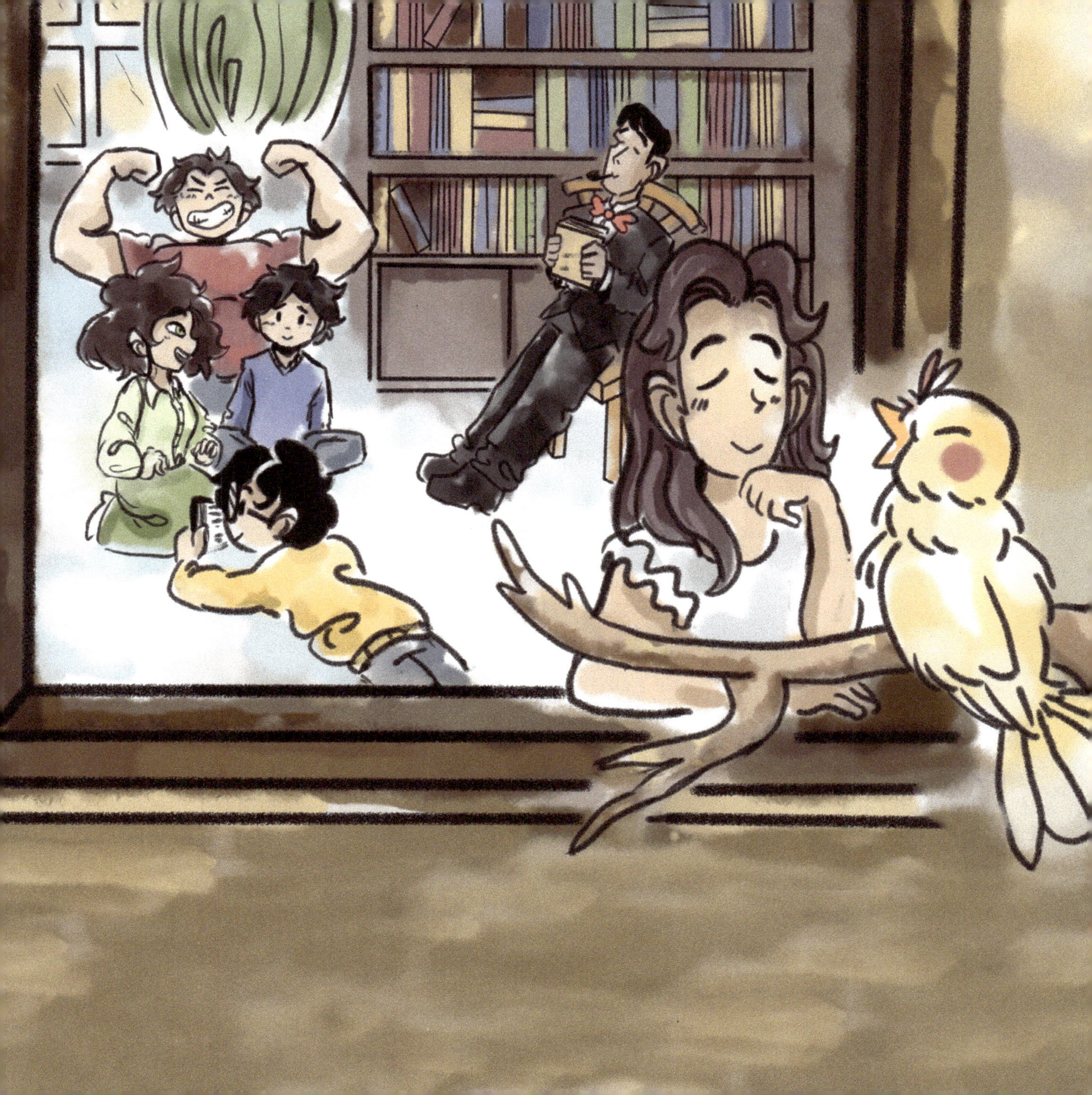

The Poros were not evil, but they wanted to protect their children from the evil that could be found outside the castle. The children had special teachers and only had their siblings as friends.

The Poro family always made sure to remain close to the village by organizing an annual banquet every early autumn.

The last banquet organized by the Poro family had gathered the inhabitants of the Mouchi village and the neighboring villages. This banquet was different, the Poro had chosen to announce the arrival of a new child who would be called Grace.

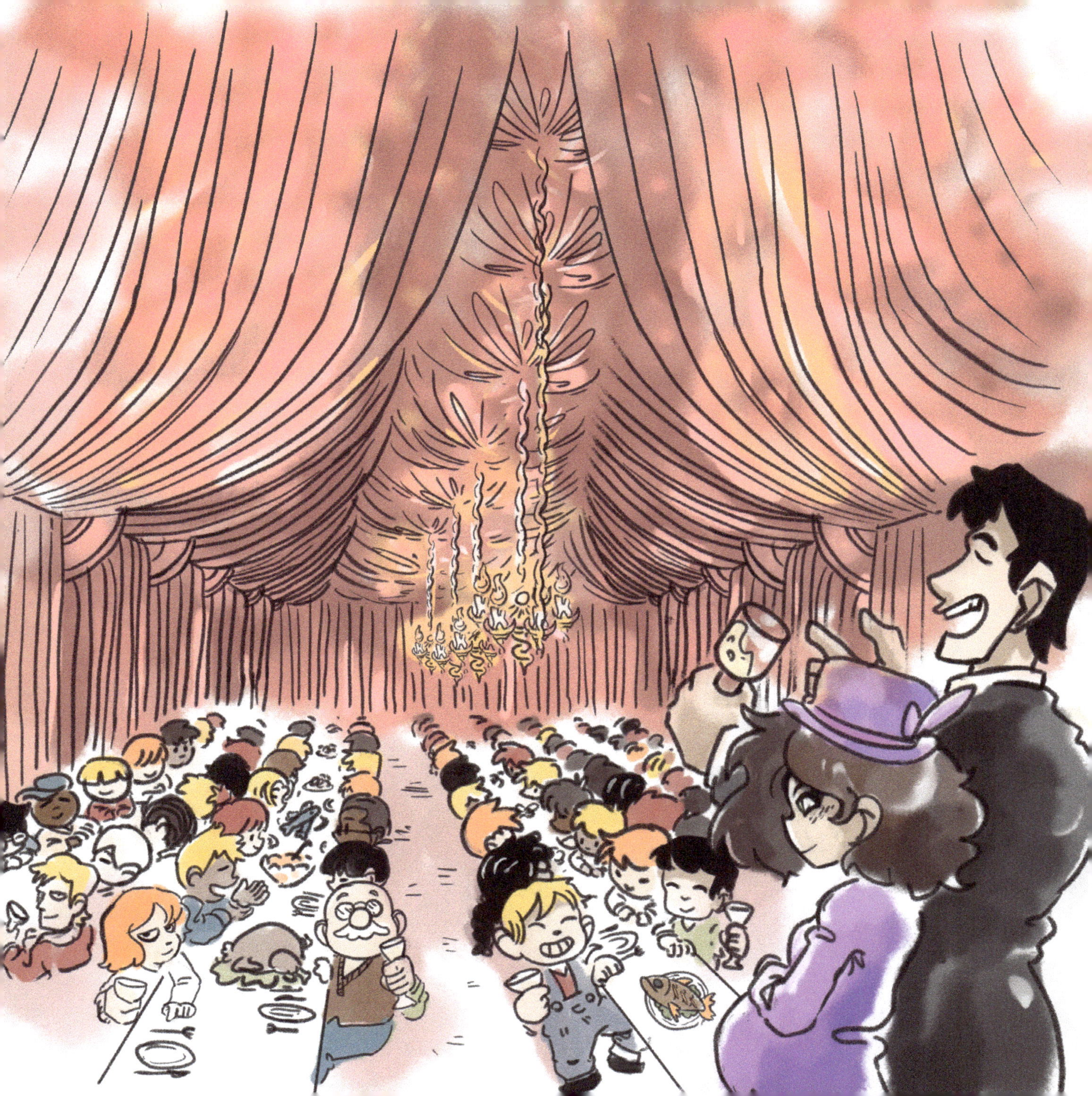

The people of the village were all very excited by the news. They were already laughing and celebrating the arrival of baby Grace, imagining the new child and wondering:

   -Was she going to be as beautiful as Maya?

   -As strong as June?

   -As smart as Jimmy?

   -As brave as Jon? Or was she going to have all the beautiful qualities of the Poro children?

   While people were toasting to the baby's arrival, Nadia's ugly sister, Foura, poured poison into the glass.

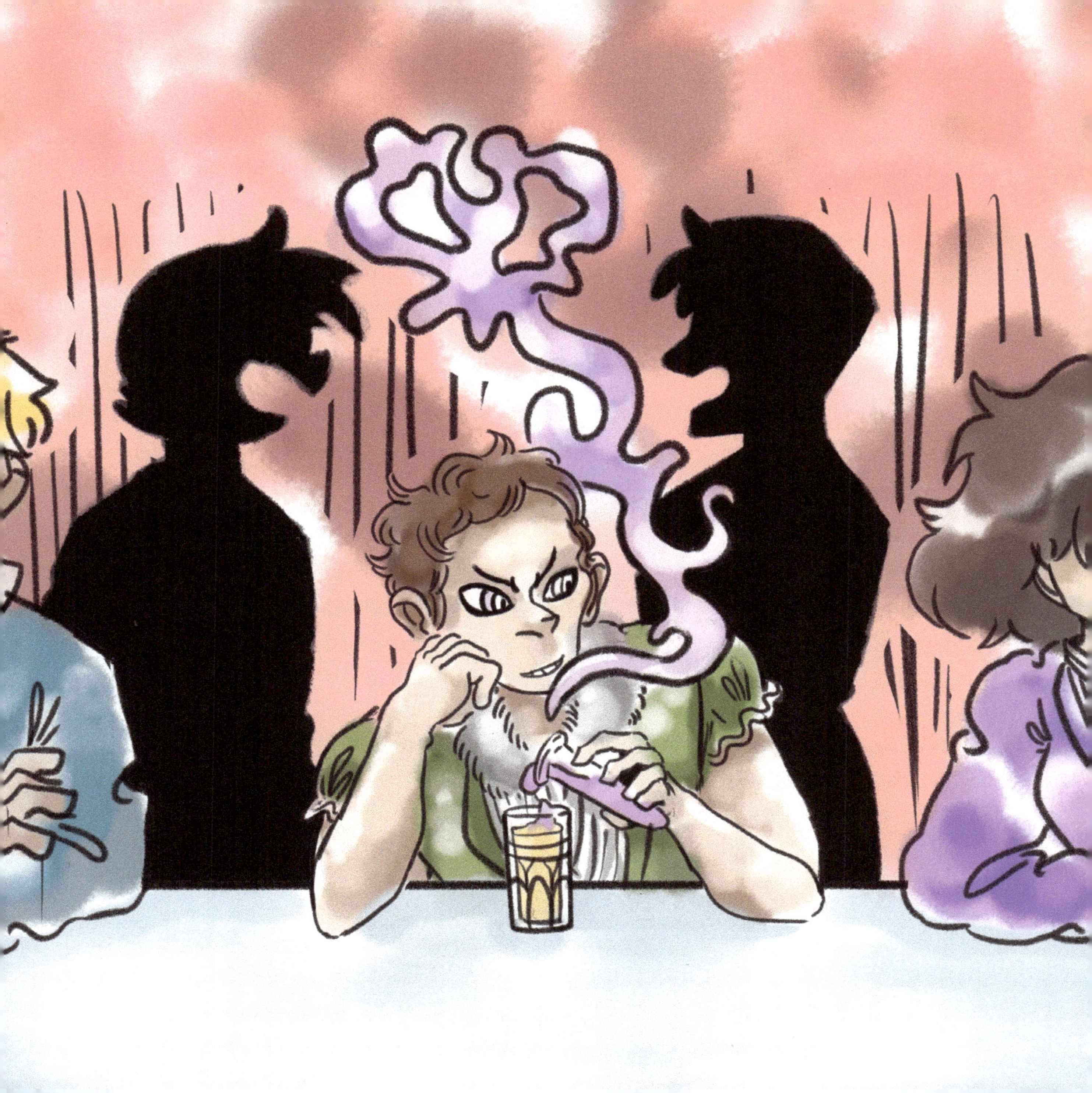

The ugly Foura had always hated Nadia, she was jealous of her beauty and would have liked to marry Abel and have children like the Poro's. She wanted to make her sister suffer and kill the baby that was in her belly.

With the poisoned glass in her hand, Nadia took a sip when suddenly, by clumsiness, Maya spilled her mother's glass on the floor. Embarrassed, Maya went to get her mother another glass of juice. Nadia smiled and kissed her daughter on the forehead.

Foura left the castle satisfied and headed for the Anca village, the village she lives in, thinking that Nadia had drunk the whole poisoned glass…

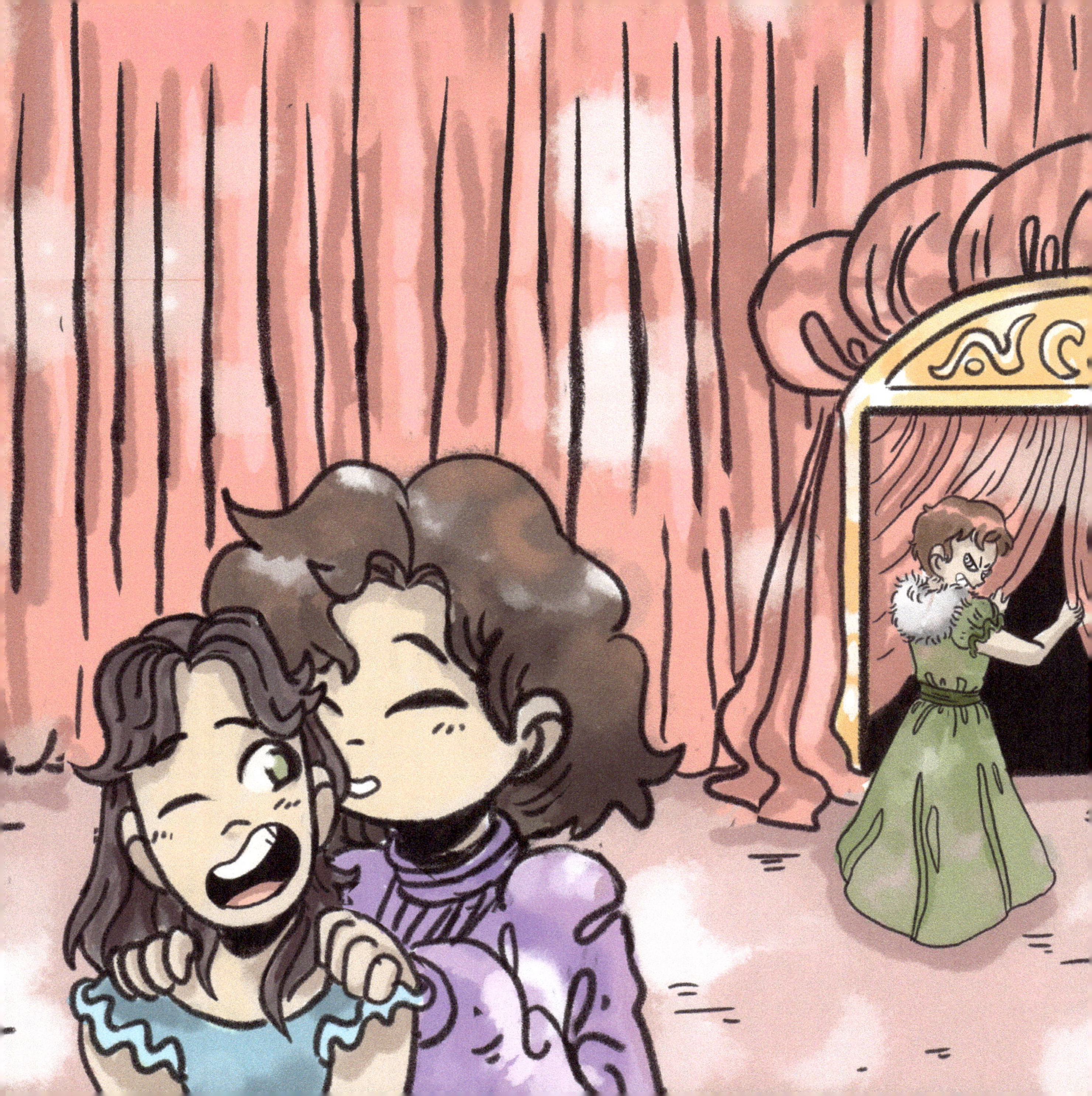

On a cold winter evening, one of the coldest the Mouchi Village had known, Grace was born… The village cleric took Grace in his arms and looked at the baby that would be the youngest of the Poros. His expression suddenly changed and his reaction was unexpected.

Head down, he announced to the parent that Nadia gave birth to a different baby, a baby with no hair, and whose eyes were being eaten by the eyelids:

-The baby looked like none of her brothers, nor her sister Maya. You gave birth to a demon!

-A demon? questioned Nadia and Abel, not understanding what was going on. They had never done anything wrong, on the contrary, they were always generous and devoted to their neighbors.

Why them? Why was such a curse placed on them? What had they done to deserve this?

The parents were crying and blaming each other:

-It's your fault, Abel, I'm sure! cried Nadia.

-No, it's yours, she was in your belly. You must be cursed, answered Abel.

-ENOUGH! shouted the religious man. It's nobody's fault, we can save your daughter. Leave the village on the eve of the fall. Go and look for a cure.

-What are we going to do until fall?

-Get to know your daughter. Spend time with her. I will visit you on the 30th of every month.

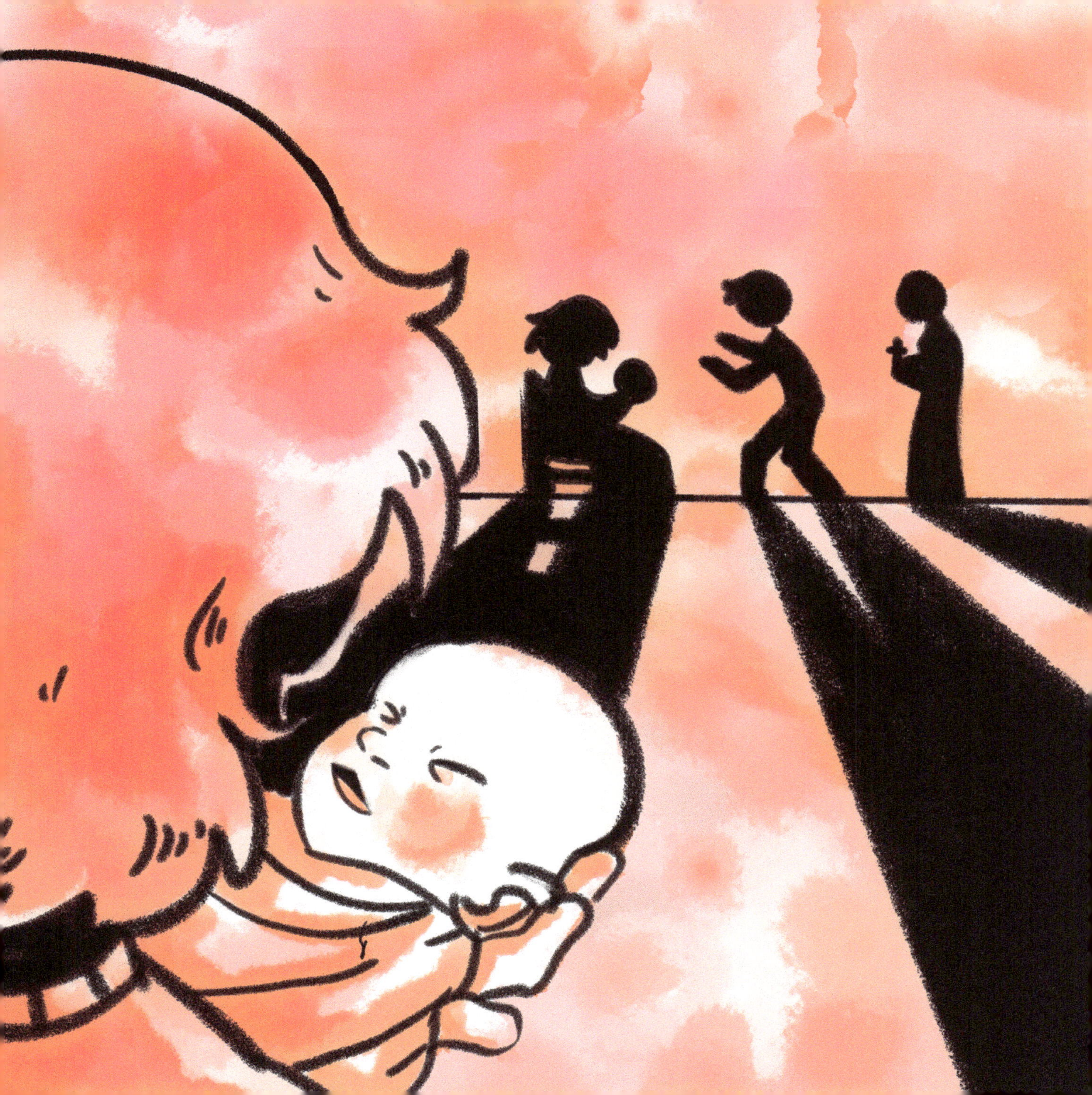

Not wanting the child to be known in the village, the Poro family and the cleric decided to keep the birth of little Grace a secret.

The months passed, the color of the leaves changed and Grace grew, she did not speak and always had a void look in her eyes. No emotions could be read on her face.

Nadia and Abel gathered their children in the family room and made them promise to always protect their sister and not to treat her differently. The three very sensitive brothers cried at their parents' words. They knew they had a long journey ahead of them.

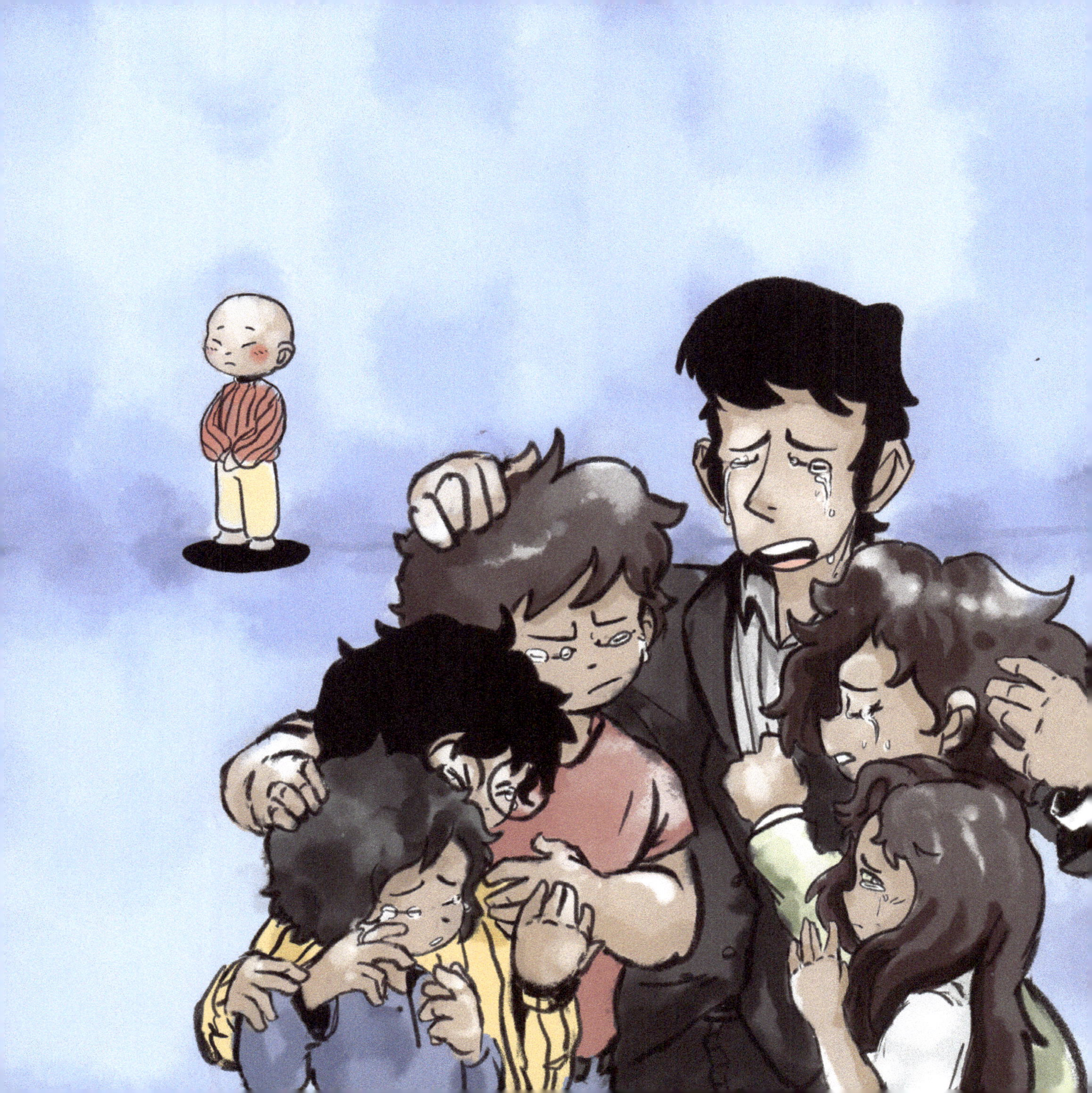

Maya approached Grace and did not understand how she was different from her. Grace had a nose, a mouth, and ears like the rest of her siblings.

She saw her sister as a fairy who could simply not be understood. That's when she had the idea to imagine a language that only the two sisters could understand. She spent all her time with Grace, playing with her even though her hairless sister did not seem to understand the world around her.

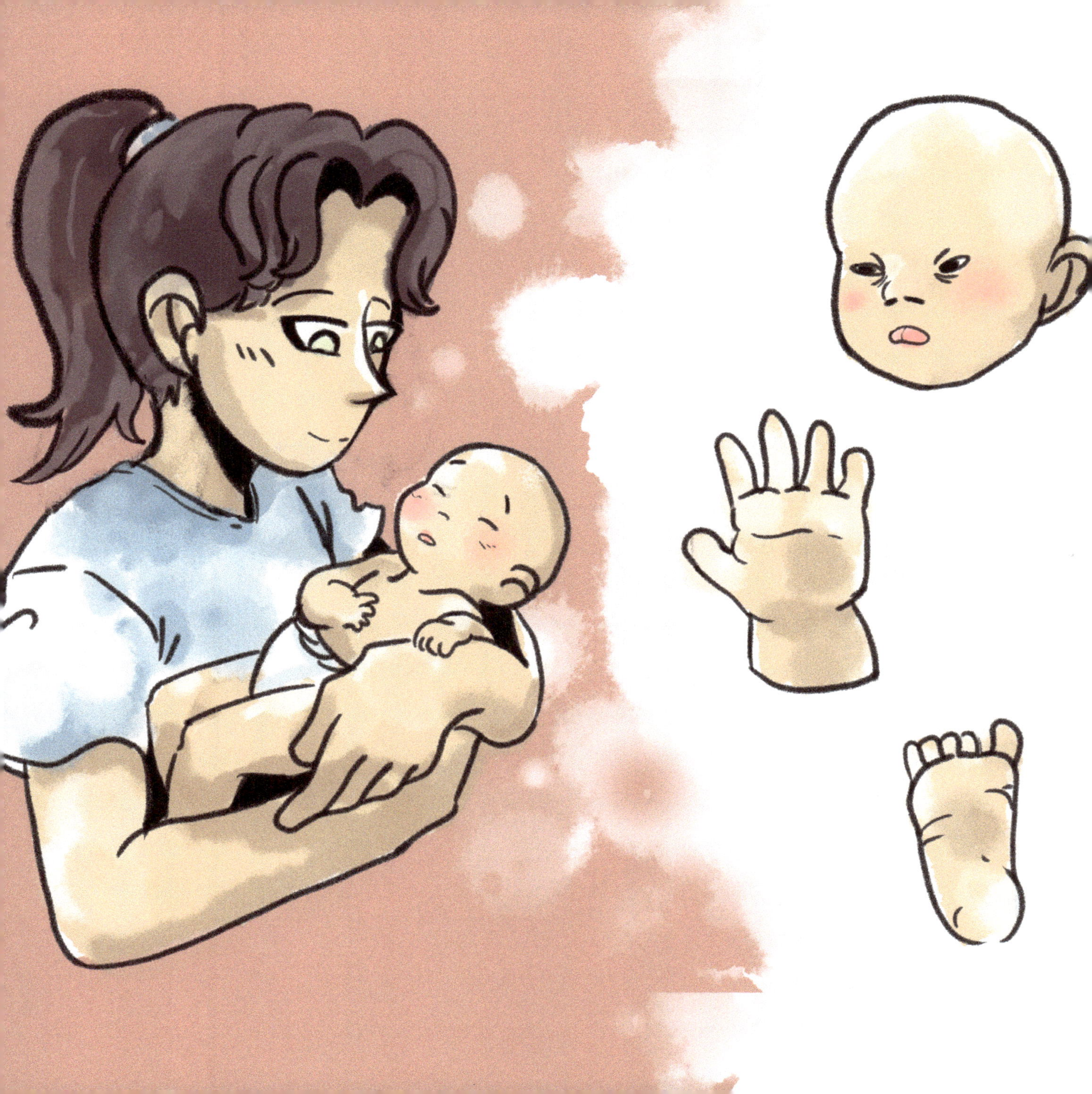

The day before autumn arrived and the parents went in quest of a cure for their daughter.

When summer arrived, the three brothers decided to leave the castle to search for their parents. They entrusted Grace to their sister and forbade her to leave the castle.

Years have passed, Nadia and Abel did not come back in the castle and the brothers had disappeared. The Poro family had almost been forgotten by the villagers.

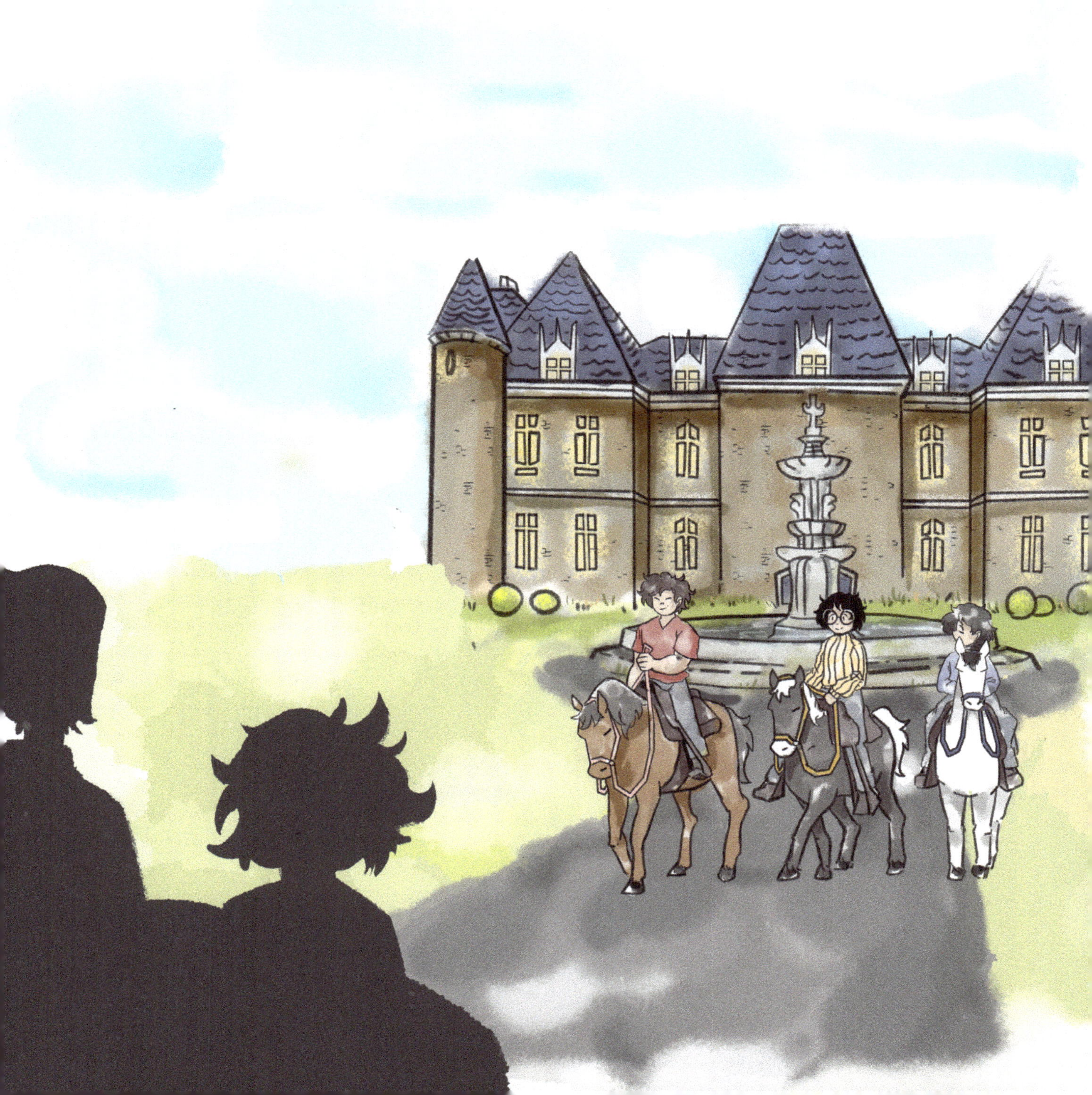

Maya had managed to teach Grace a few words and the two sisters were able to communicate. One morning when Maya opened the window, she saw a pretty special bird she had never seen before. It was an azure bird with pink and green stripes. Its whistle was simply beautiful. The bird stood at her window for a few minutes and flew away to the Mouchi village.

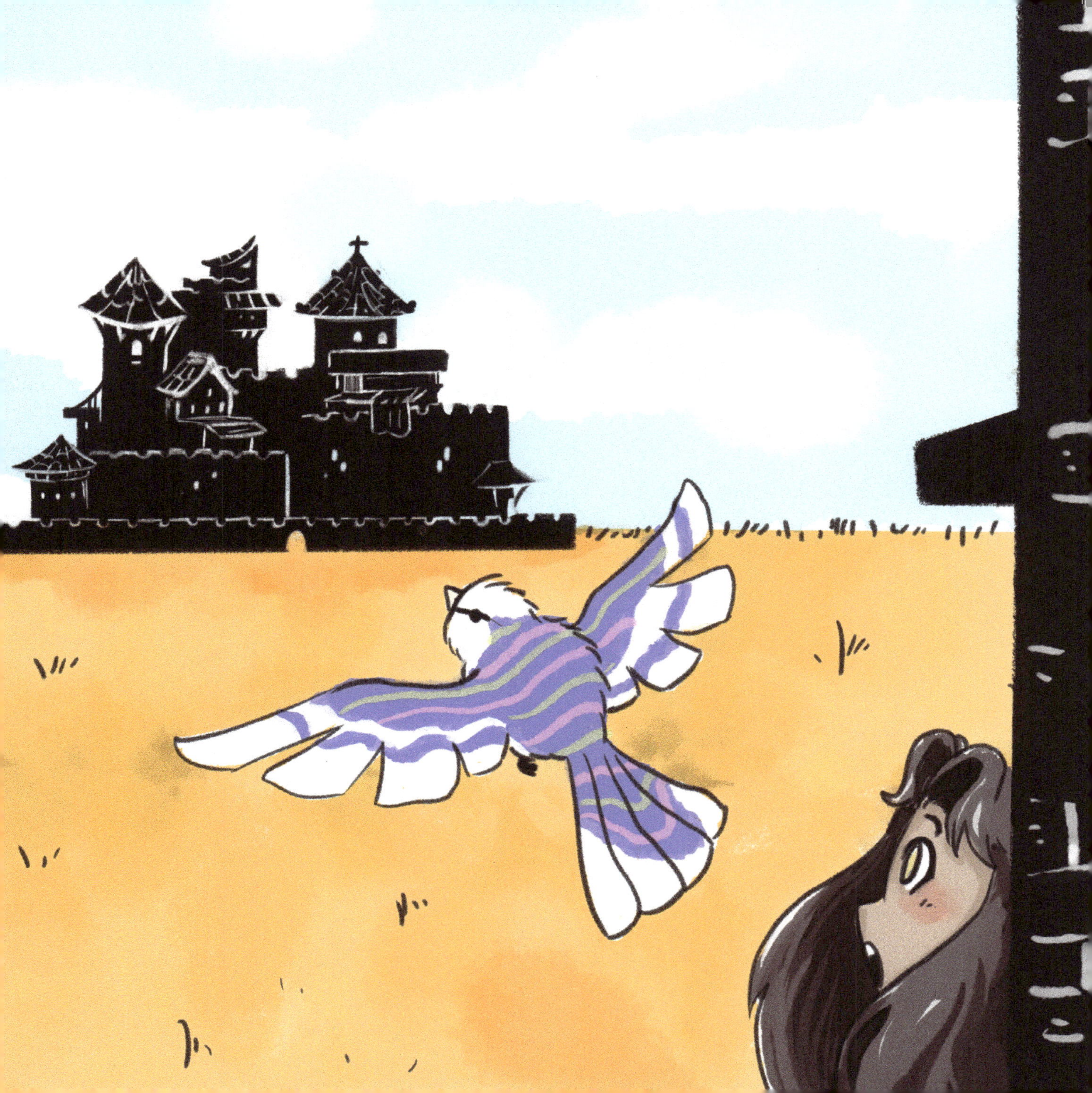

Maya wanted to follow him or at least to do as he did and discover this village. She dressed her sister and prepared to go down to the village.

After all, her brothers were still not there and the ban on going to the village was several years old!

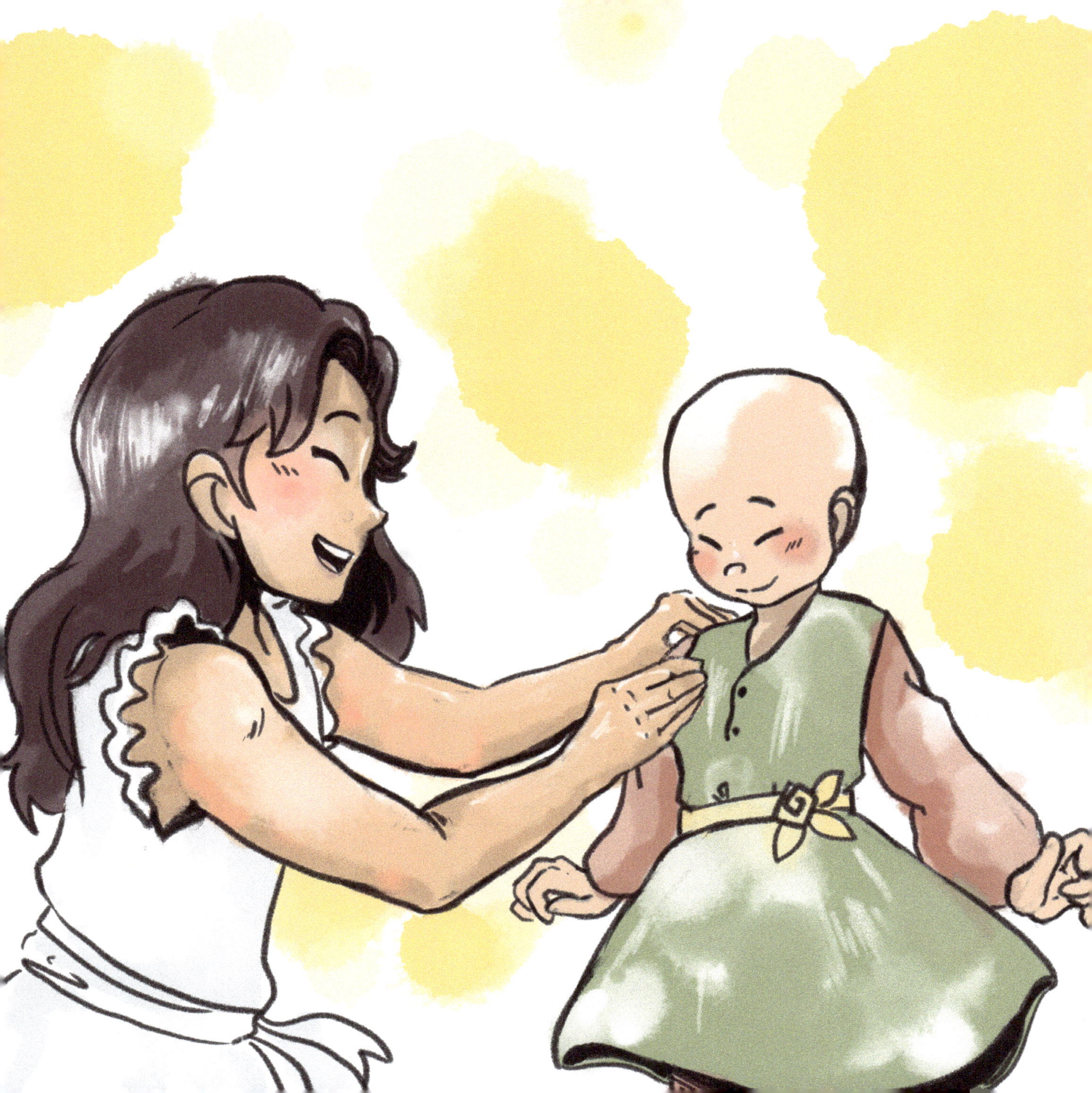

The two sisters arrived innocently in the village. Their arrival was quickly noticed… the village had become petrified.

Some were dazzled by Maya's beauty and others were terrified by the girl with no hair. Maya paid no attention and kept walking, stopping at bakery to buy some cakes. Bewitched by her beauty, the baker offered her a bag full of sweets.

"I haven't seen you for years, but your beauty is unchanged. You look a lot like your mother, but you have your father's smile," said the baker.

The baker's words put a smile on her face.

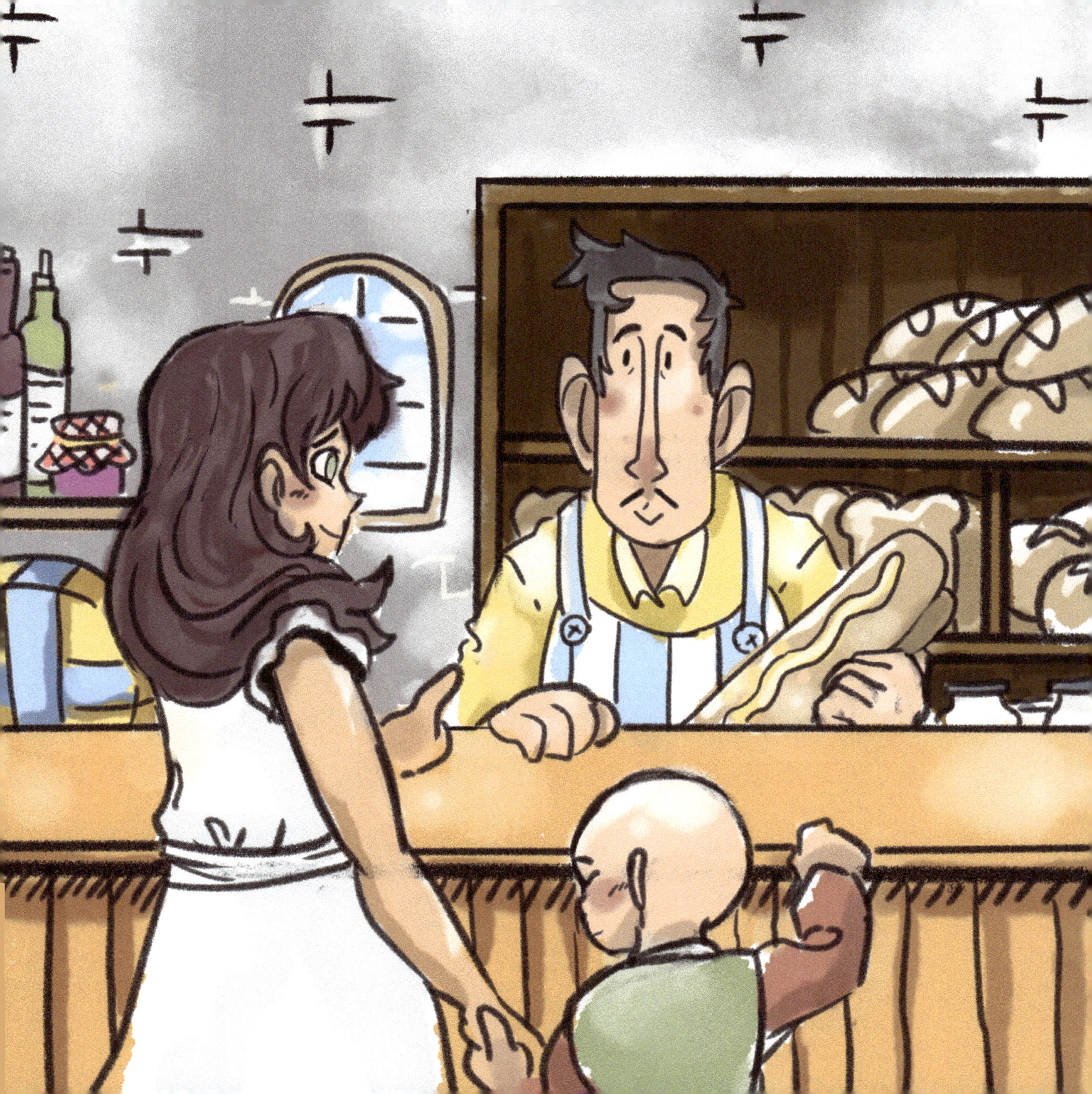

When the baker's grandson saw little Grace, he screamed with fear. The villagers began to talk, whispering rumors. You could see in their faces that they feared the young Grace.

They pointed to the hairless sister and said:

-Who is this girl who has no hair? Is she the last daughter of the Poros?

-We thought they were hiding her because her beauty was as exceptional as Maya's.

-She is a monster, look at her! She has no hair.

-It's a monster, I'm sure she doesn't have a soul.

-It's a witch, its eyes are small.

-It's a monster.

Gahwa & Bread

Sweet Grace was in her bubble and didn't realize that people feared her. She didn't even understand what was going on, so she started waving at people. Maya laughed. She thought it was funny that people were afraid of her sister. She didn't understand why they couldn't see her how she sees her.

Suddenly, a villager pushed the girl with no hair and made her fall to the ground.

Mad with anger, Maya took a stick and in panic, she scraped her hand, pushed the villager away and shouted:

-Nobody touches my sister, I will kill anyone who tries to hurt her.

Then a wing suddenly appeared on Maya's back, a wing as white as snow. A single wing that did not allow her to fly. The villagers were stunned by what they had just seen.

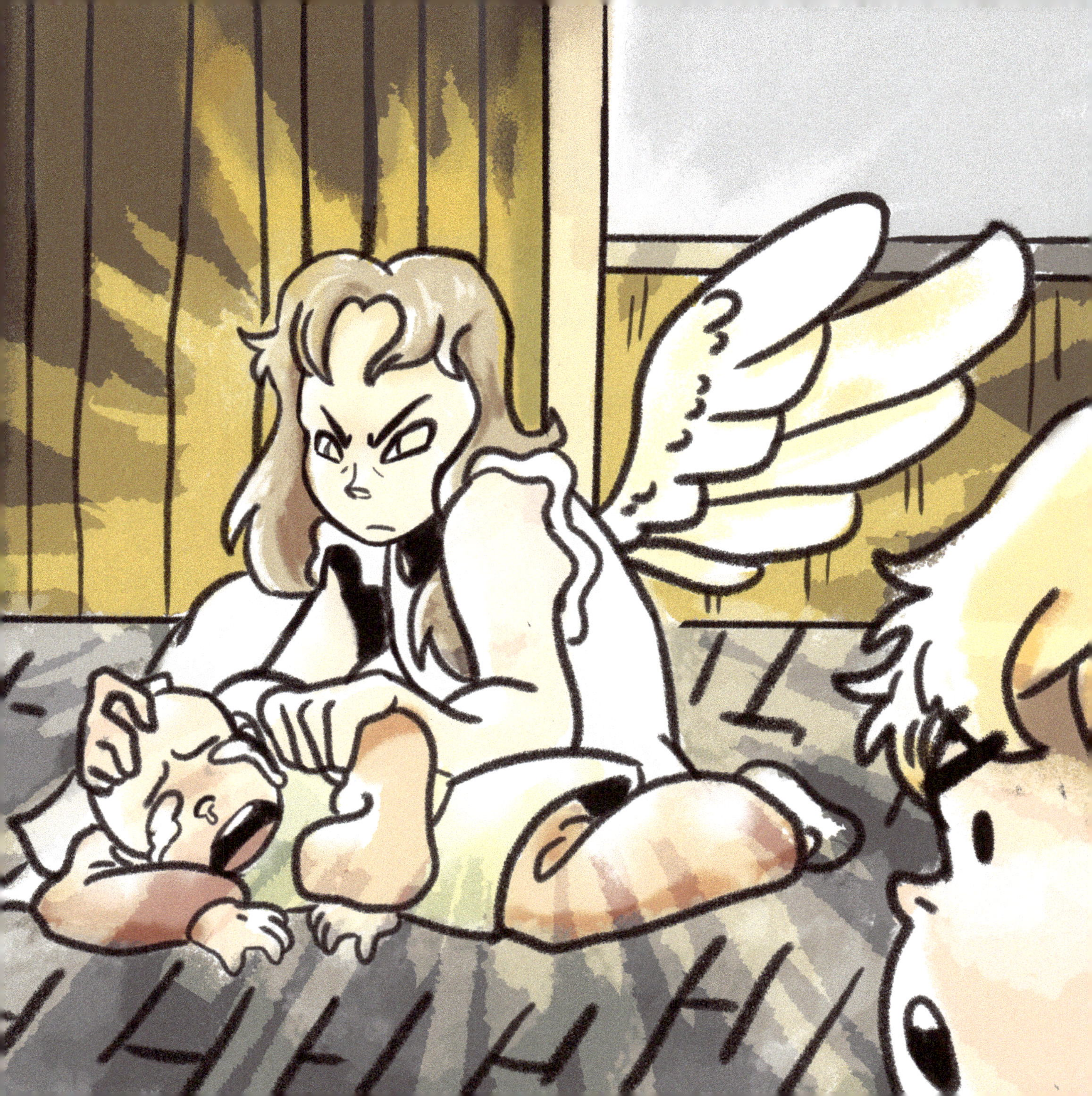

Maya took advantage of this moment to take Grace by the hand and ran at full speed towards the castle.

The villagers wasted no time to ring the church bell, gathering weapons and storming the castle to kill the two sisters.

Torch and pitchfork in hand, they destroyed the gate and shouted:

-Let's kill the witch-sisters.

-We must kill them!

-Our crop failed; they must have cursed them.

-They spread misfortune everywhere and make our children cry.

-Yes, let's kill the witch-sisters.

-Let's burn them.

-They must have killed their mother.

-And their brothers must have run away in fear.

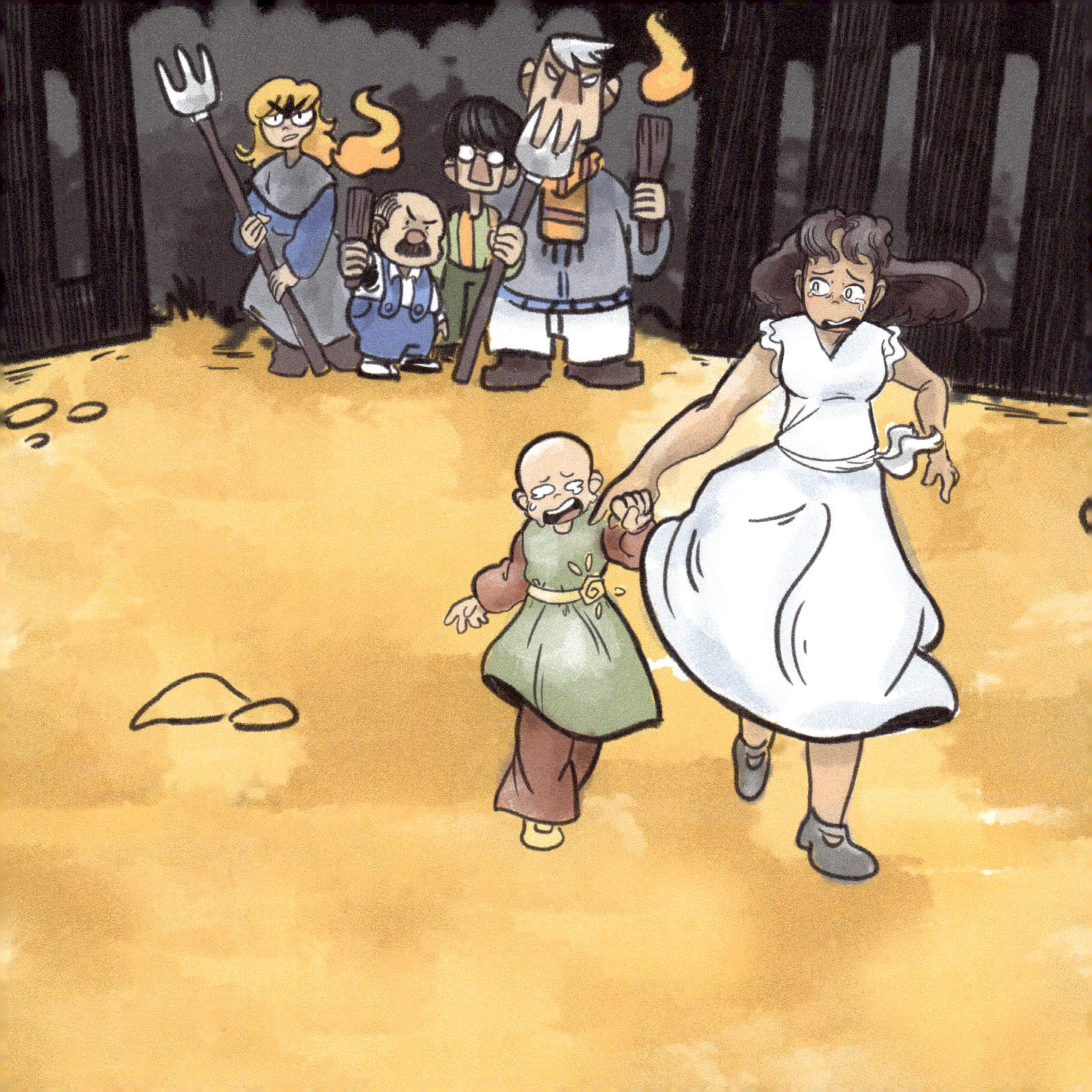

Grace became anxious as she heard the villagers screaming, looked out the window and saw terrifying expressions on the faces of the villagers as they tried to enter the castle. She sat down on the floor and began to cry and hit her face.

Maya smiled and put her hand on her sister's heart for a few seconds and tried to reassure her. She picked up Grace and carried her on her back. They walked through the castle's underground passageway that led to the Sira Forest.

The villagers successfully destroyed the front door of the castle and searched for the two sisters, but failed to find them. They realized that they had run away. They left the area and locked the castle doors.

The two sisters walked towards the forest. Maya said to her sister:

-Maya and Grace are going to look for Mom and Dad. Okay? Grace is not afraid. Grace is a brave girl.

-Yes, okay, Maya, Grace, Mommy, Daddy.

-Yes, sweetheart that's right!

They held hands and set off on a journey to find their parents.

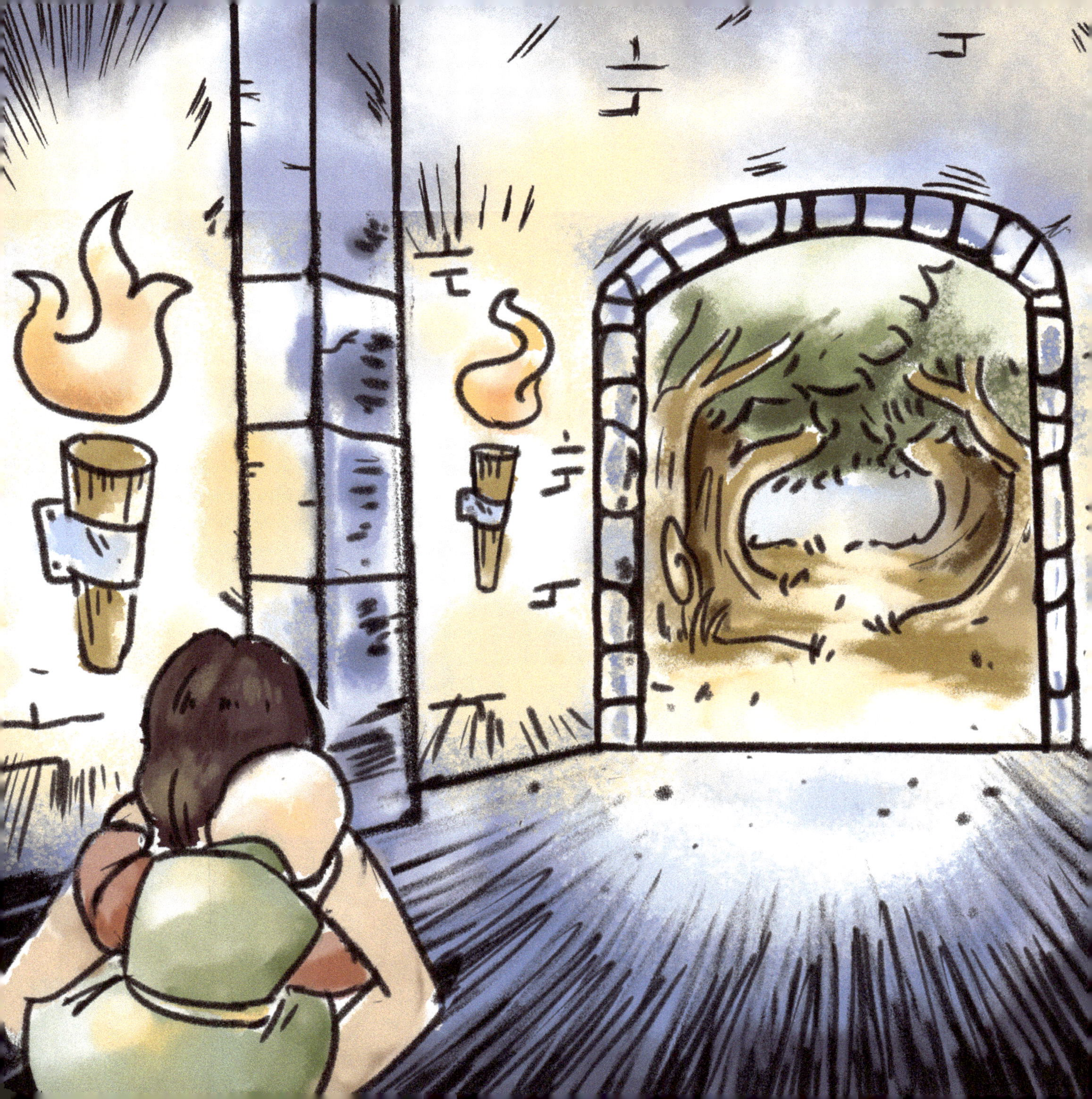

Upon entering the forest, the sisters found a crying Centaur curled up in the snow. The girl with no hair asked the Centaur:

-Why are you crying?

-I came to join my human friend, but I dropped the magic charm that could turn me into a human. If she sees me like this, she will be scared and no longer want to be my friend. The centaur had shed all of his tears, he was beating his chest to show his sadness. When Grace saw this, she began to imitate him and started crying and beating her chest.

The centaur immediately stopped crying, looked at her and said:

-Why are you crying?

-I… I… I am crying because you are afraid of yourself and it makes me very sad.

The Centaur looked at Grace and observed her more closely.

Maya approached him with a smile and said:

-My sister is as unique as you are, look at her, she's beautiful! Don't change to please your friend, she will love you as you are.

Because of Grace's tears, the snow began to melt, revealing the magic charm that had been hidden underneath.

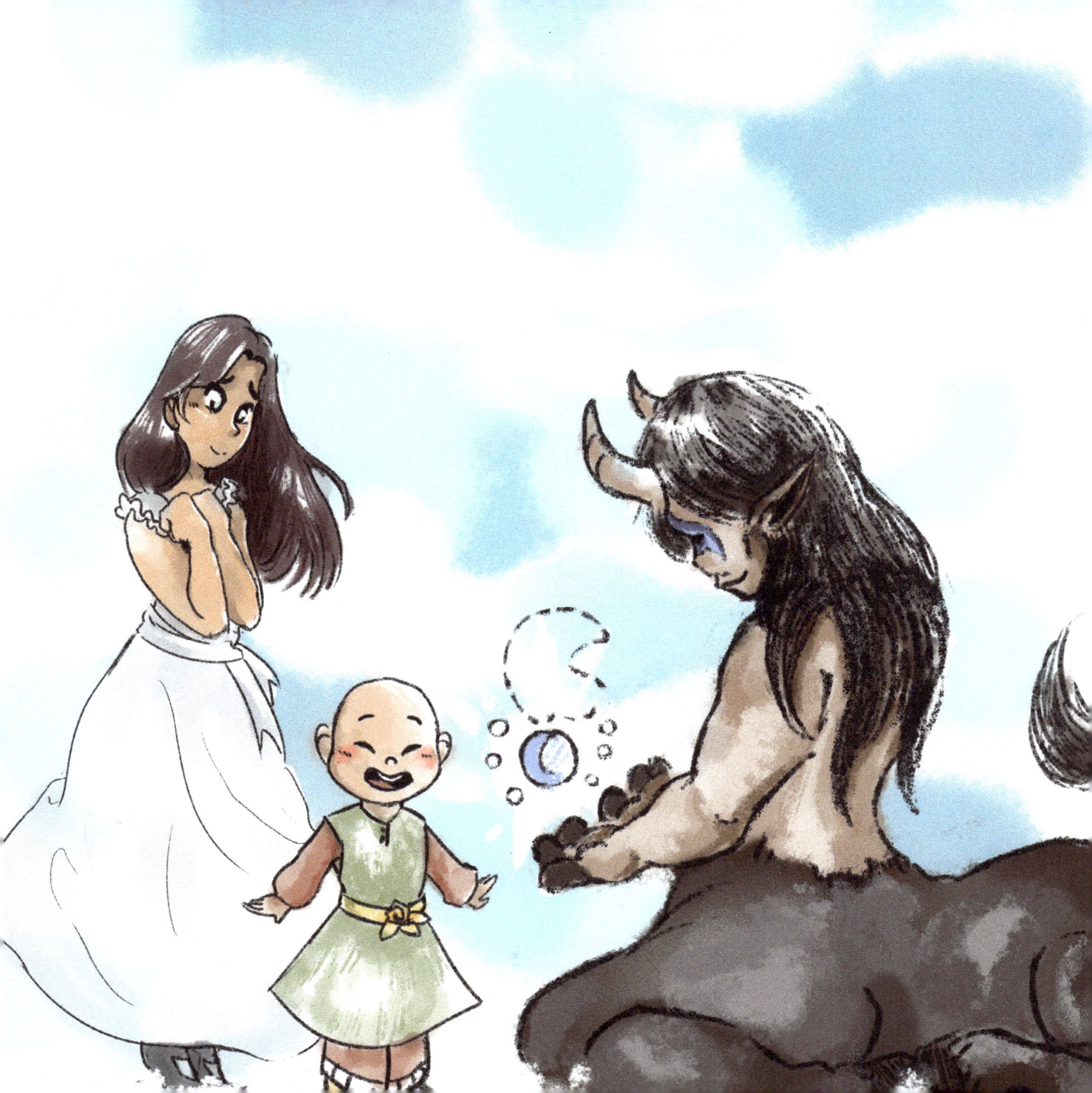

The centaur grabbed the magic charm and gazed at Grace.

He decided to give her the talisman and said:

-You are right, I should not be afraid of myself. Keep this talisman as a souvenir of our meeting. It won't change your shape, but it will remind you of our encounter and remind you that it is important to always believe in yourself.

Maya smiled, wiped away her sister's tears and placed her hand on her heart for a few seconds. She took Grace in her arms and carried her on her back. The two young women left the Centaur and continued their journey.

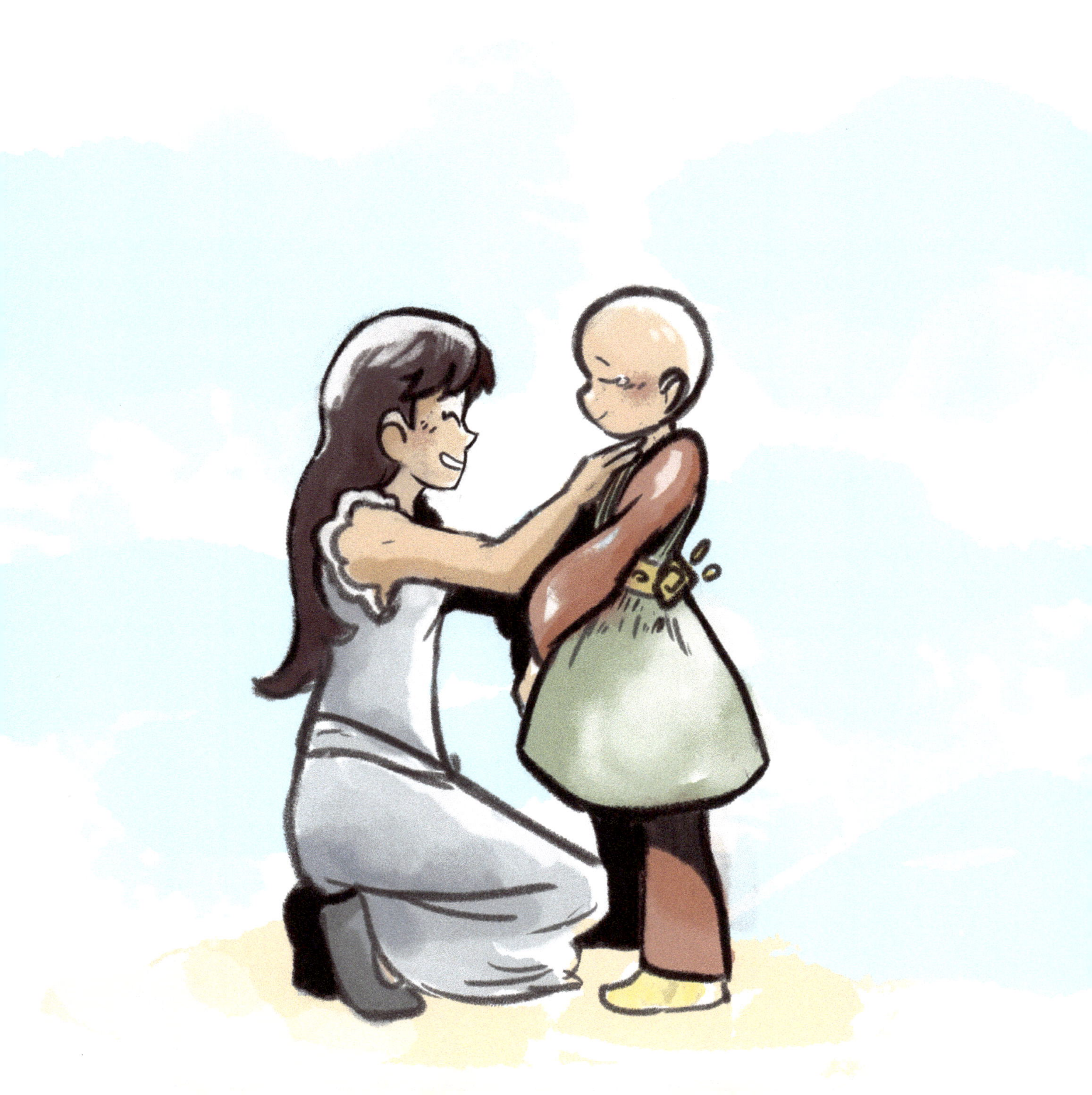

The two sisters continued to move forward in their journey, dazzled by the beauty of nature. The flowers smiled at them and the ants let them pass. While on their quest, the two girls heard a beautiful song. It was so beautiful that they could not resist and they decided to follow the direction of the song and came upon a lamb. Maya asked the lamb:

-Why are you singing when you are surrounded by thorns?

-It's the only way I can be seen.

-But it's dangerous and no one is watching you but us. Your beautiful voice should be enough. You don't need to put yourself in danger.

Grace approached the thorny flowers and began to sing near the lamb: "I'm a girl with no hair and everyone is looking at me. I'm going to help you."

When Grace began to sing after the lamb, all the animals of the forest began to approach. The crowd looked at the spectacle and asked:

-Who is this monster?

-What kind of monster is that?

-The poor thing is really horrible.

-The lamb has a beautiful voice!

-But look at the girl with no hair.

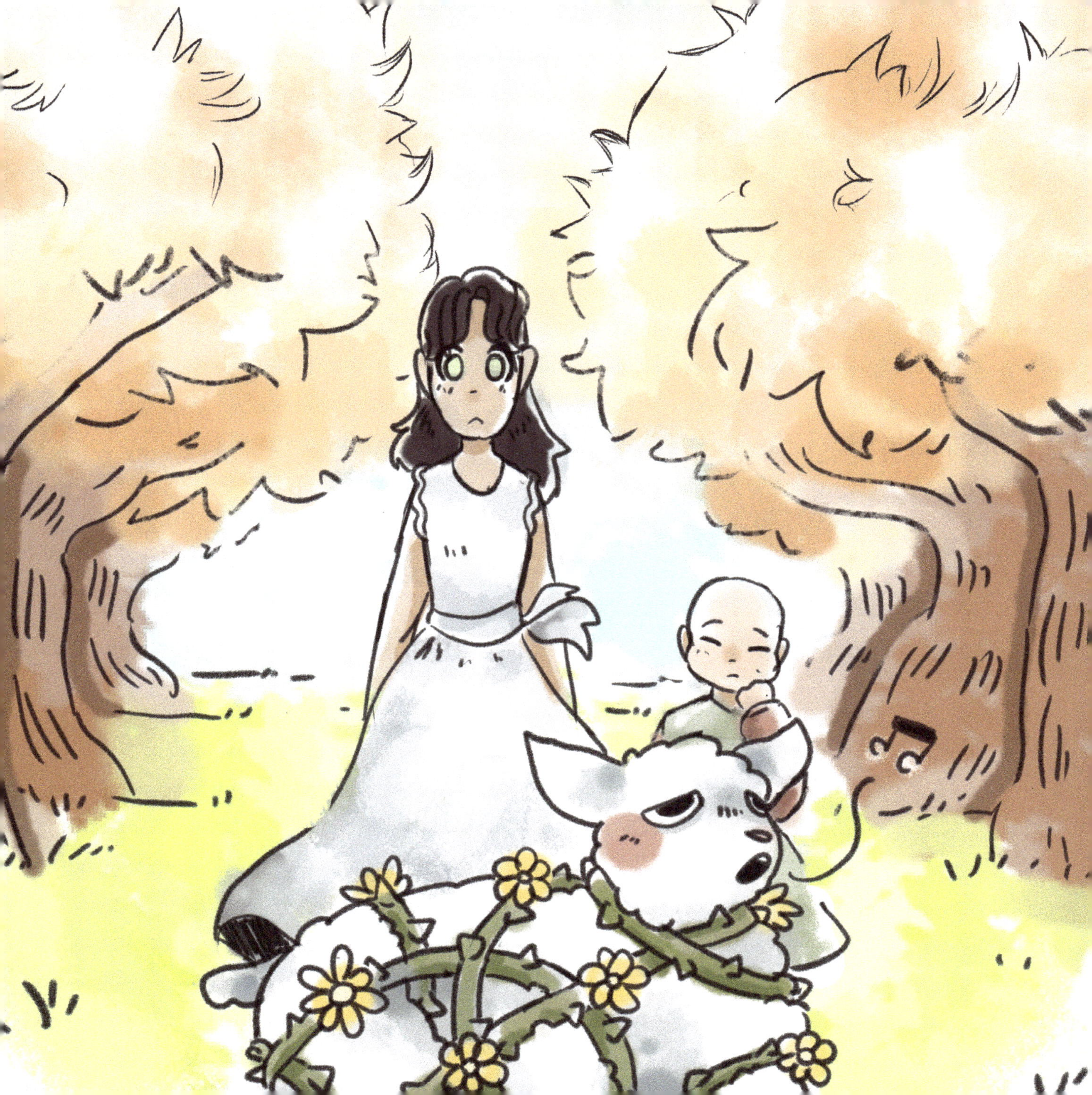

Maya joined her sister and the crowd applauded her beauty. The lamb smiled at the two sisters and said:

-Thank you, now I understand that the crowd is curious. They can be horrified or dazzled by what they don't know. Take this thorny flower with you, it will remind you of our meeting.

Maya smiled and placed her hand on her sister's heart for a few seconds. She took Grace in her arms and carried her on her back and continued on with her journey.

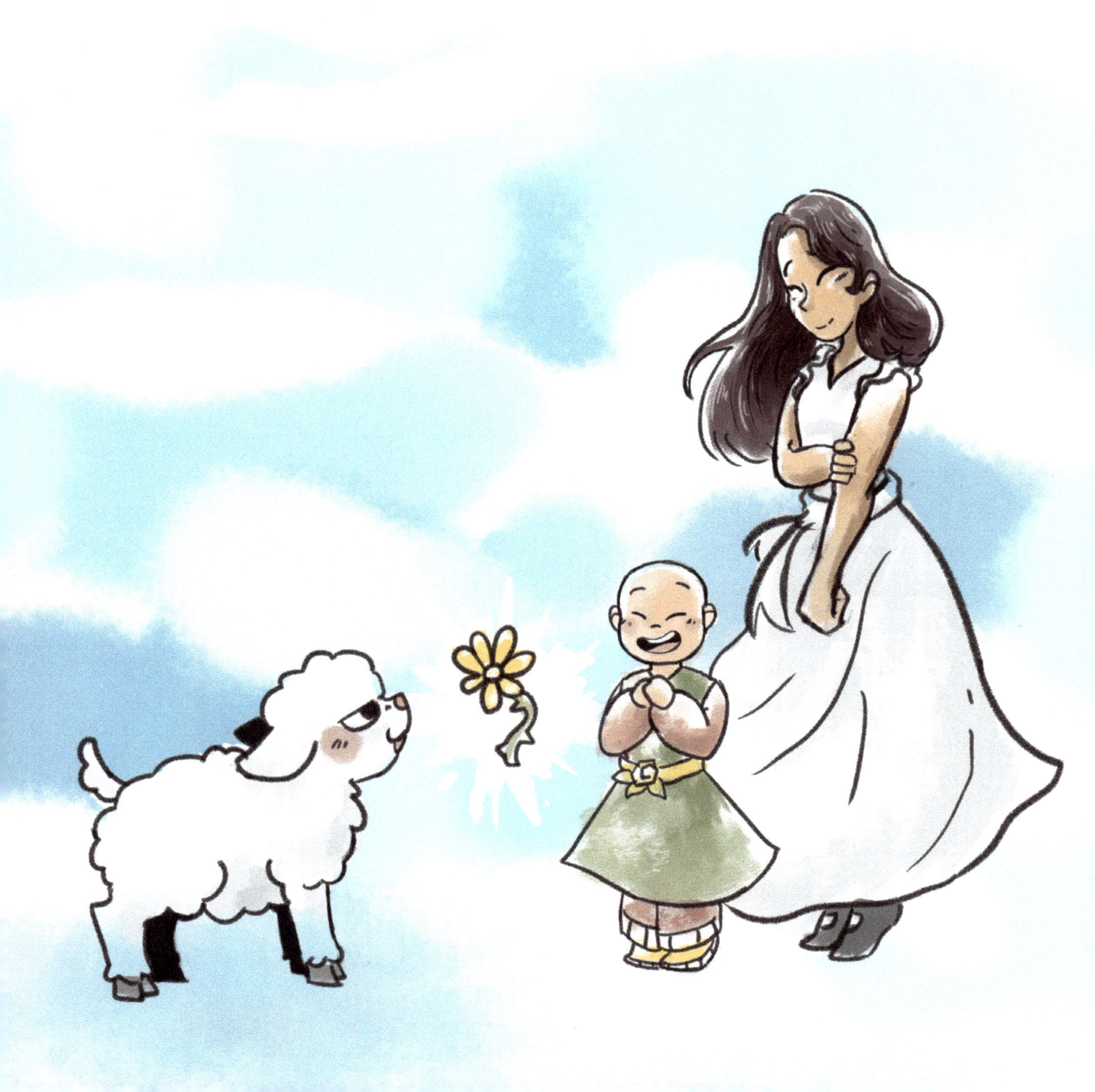

Suddenly, an evil chimera appeared in front of them.

Grace ran towards it:

-Oh, you're beautiful, Maya look at the dog!

-How dare you little human. How dare you touch me and confuse me with a vulgar dog! I am Mene, the chimera of the Sira forest! Everyone fears me, shouted the chimera.

-Wow! You are beautiful hairy dog, Maya, Maya look dog.

Maya held back her laughter and took her sister by the hand while she apologized to the chimera and tried to continue her way.

The chimera shook the ground and roared to make the two sisters fall.

-You're not nice, said Grace.

-I am a chimera, why should I be nice?

-Why should you be a bad dog, good dog, good dog?

Speechless, the chimera remained silent for a moment and then said:

-Everyone fears me, people scream before I even roar. They say I am the cause of storms and shipwrecks and blame me for all kinds of natural disasters.

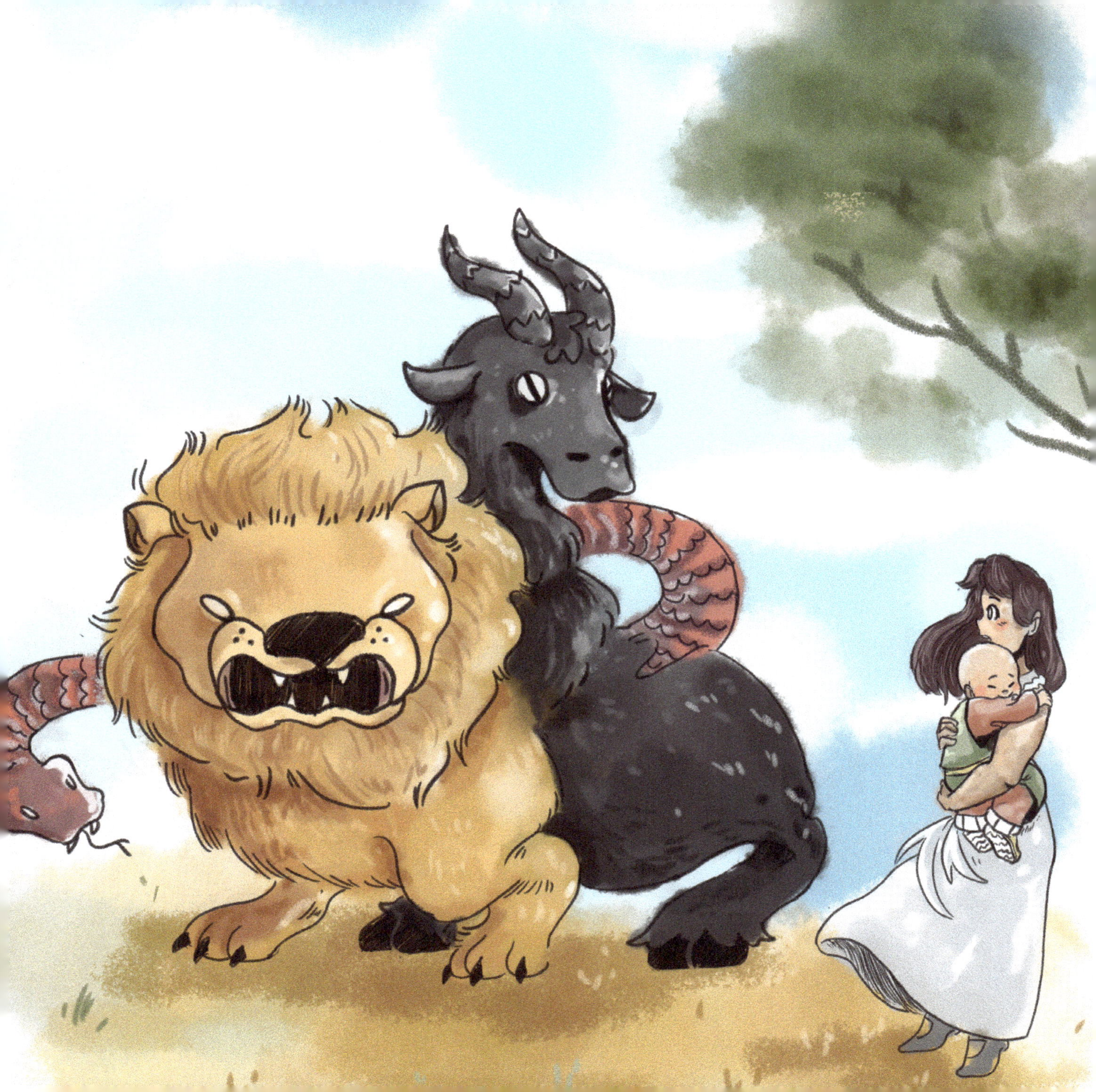

Maya smiled and said:

-Oh Mene, when the Mouchi villagers first saw my sister, they screamed monster. They claimed that it was her that caused the crop failure. She didn't change for them… I mean, even if she wanted to, she couldn't change her appearance.

Mene the chimera did not answer.

Maya placed her hand on her sister's heart for a few seconds.

She took Grace in her arms and continued on her way, leaving the chimera standing silently behind them.

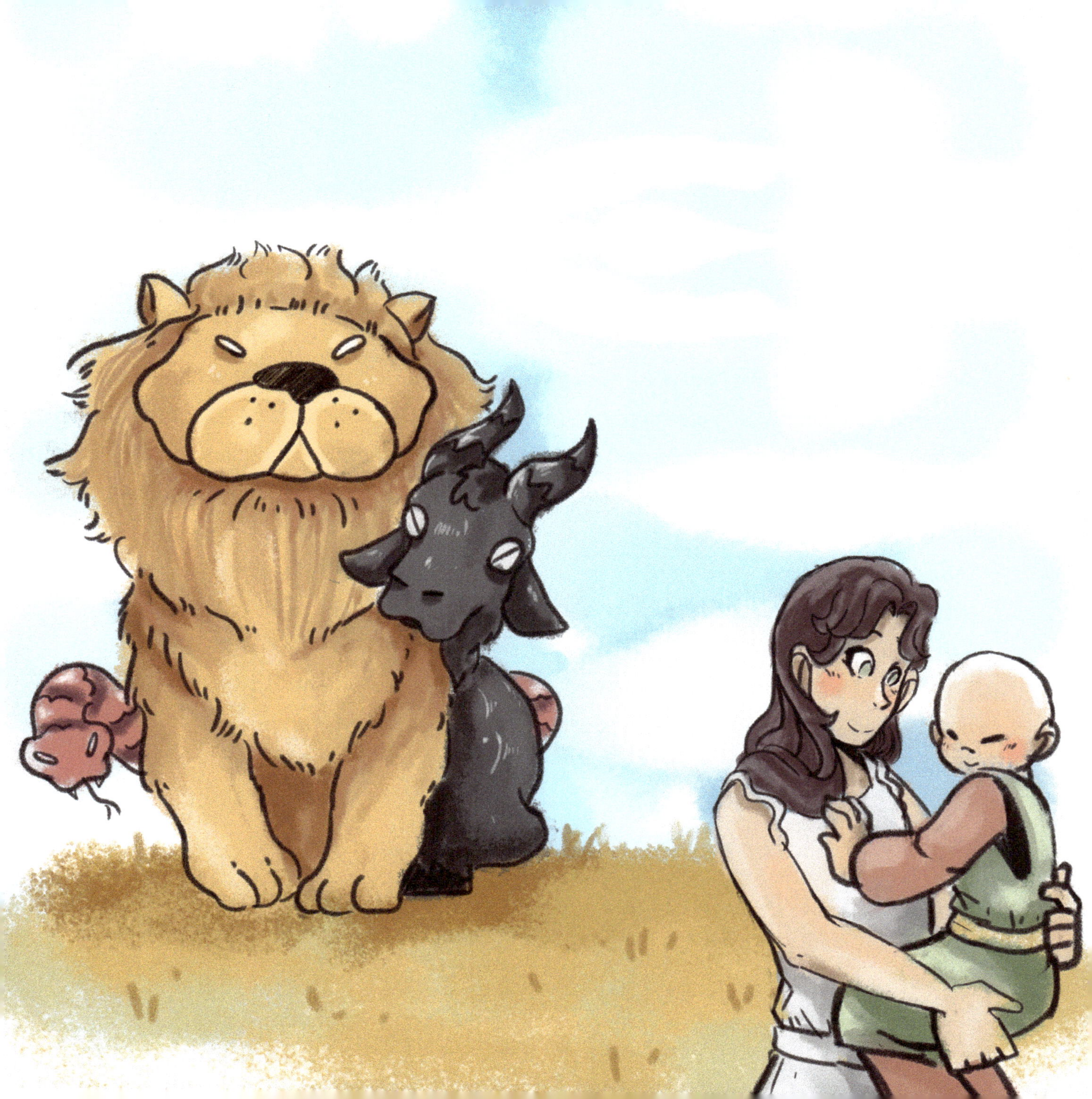

As the night fell, the sisters were still walking in the cold desert without a clue on where to go.

Fatigue set in and the sisters continued to walk. Until Grace decided to stop, impossible to make her move. Maya tried to convince her not to stop, but she was too exhausted to continue.

"You have to keep moving or you'll get even colder." She said, trying to encourage her little sister.

Grace didn't answer.

"Grace, please try to keep going for a while, maybe we'll find a place to take shelter."

The youngest sister dropped to the ground and said: "No." Maya tried to calm her down, but no result, she also bent down to her sister and hugged her with all her strength for several hours. The girl calmed down, looked at Maya and said: -Sorry Maya, sorry.

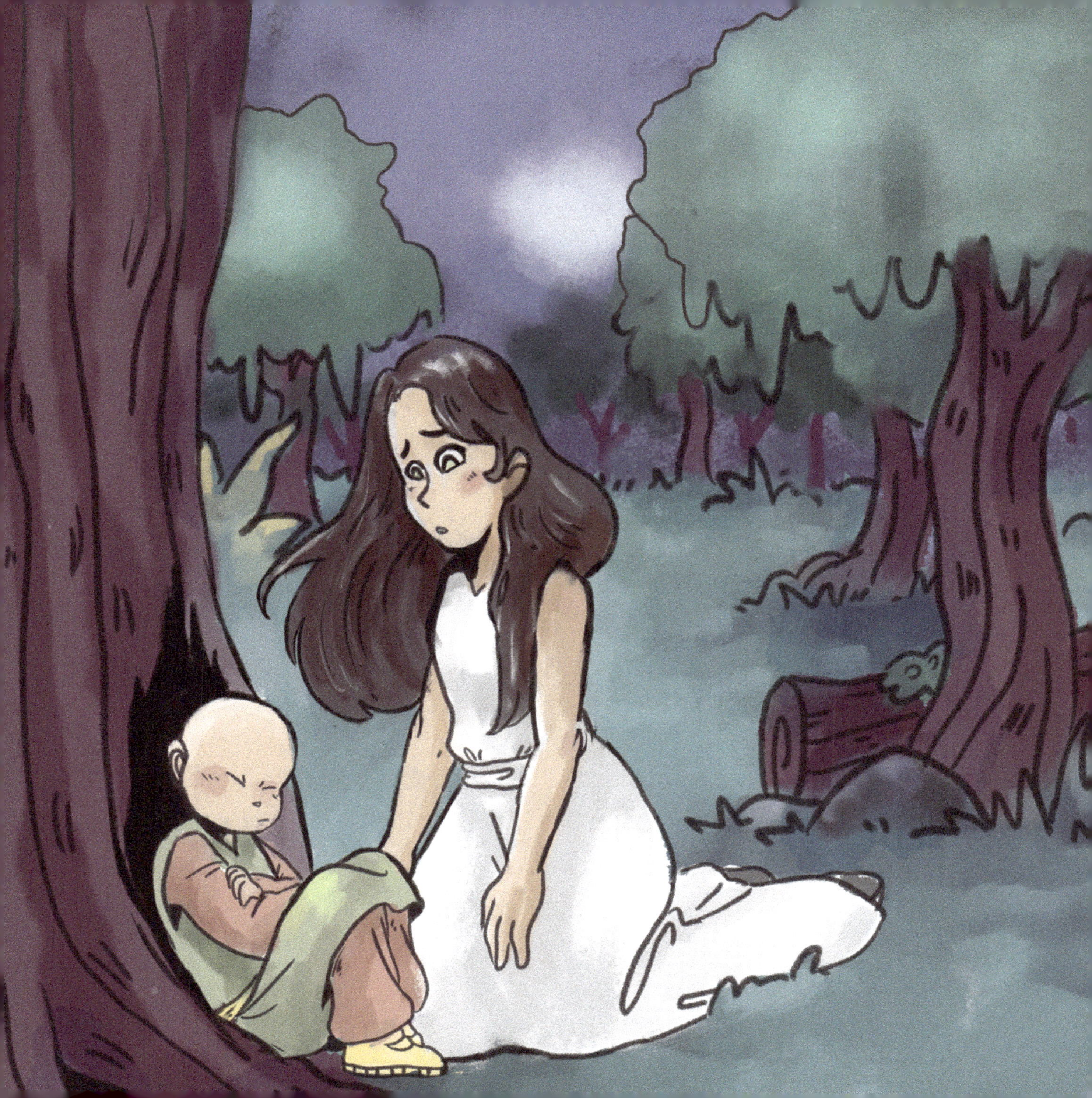

With tears in her eyes, Maya put her hand on her sister's heart for a few seconds. She took Grace in her arms and continued on her way.

Maya saw a molehill and went inside for the night. She put her sister to sleep and closed her eyes as well.

When they woke up, Maya realized that someone had locked them in the molehill. It was impossible for them to get out to continue their journey. Maya tried to remove the stone that was in the way, but didn't have enough strength. For the first time, Maya had stopped smiling. She was anxious and didn't know what to do.

Grace put her hand on her sister's heart and took her in arms and said:
- Are you okay, Maya? Are you okay?
- Yes, I am okay, Grace. I am. Maya is fine.

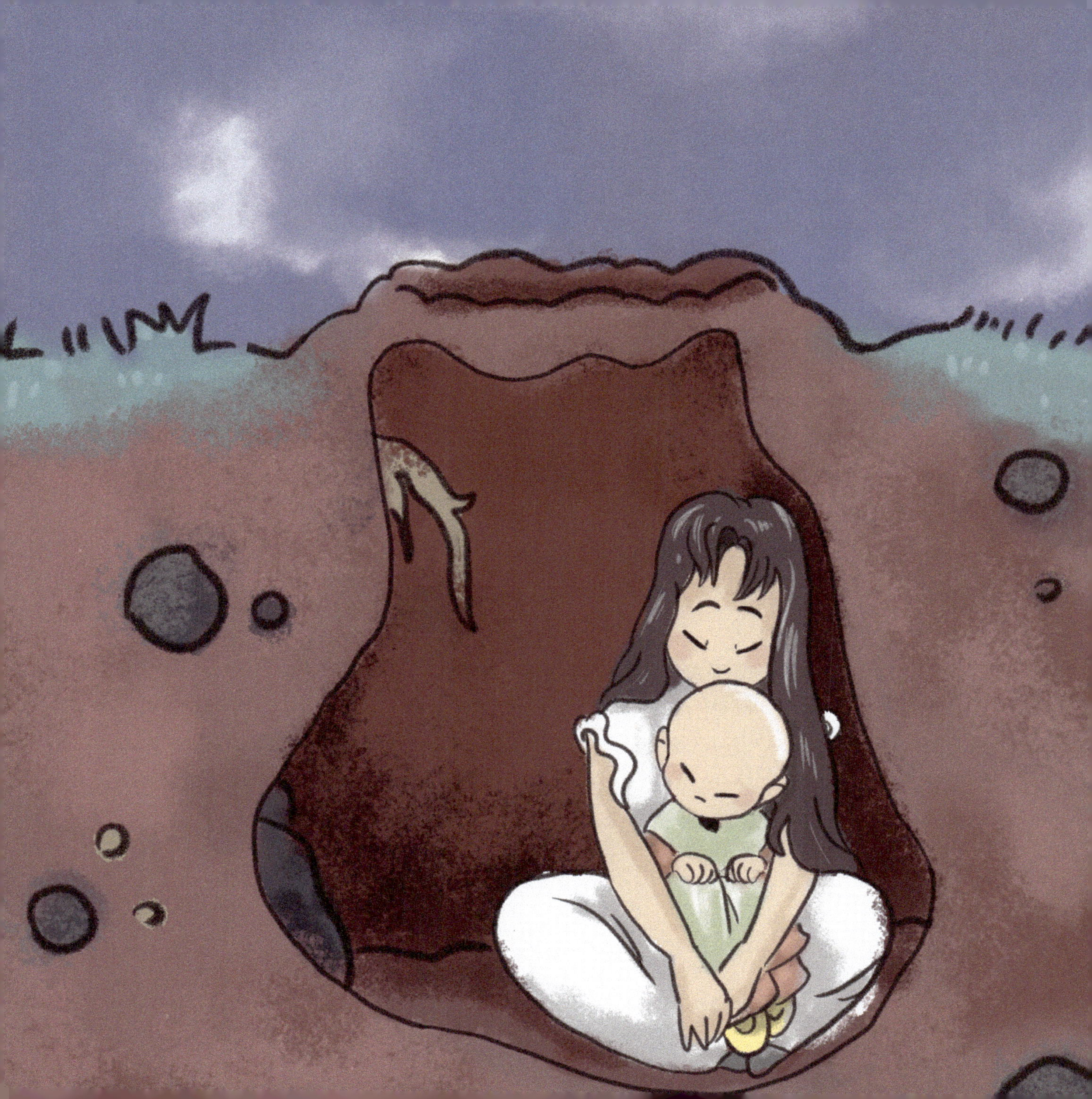

Maya touched the stone and shouted:

-Help, help us, we are in the molehill.

You could hear pats approaching the molehill. A very sharp voice said:

-Is anyone there?

-Yes! Please help us! I spent the night in the molehill with my sister, but we can't get out anymore, someone must have placed a rock by mistake.

-I can't help you. I have no paws… I can't move the rock that is blocking your way.

Talking to himself, the character with the high-pitched voice said:

"What should I do? I want to help them, but I have no paws. Is there any other way I can get into the molehill?"

The girl's voice came to him from inside the molehill.

- "It's okay, don't worry about us, we'll find a solution. As long as I am with my sister, I am fine. Good luck to you and remember that having less paws does not make you less strong. On the contrary, I think that you were so strong that life wanted to remove your paws so that there is no big difference between you and other people."

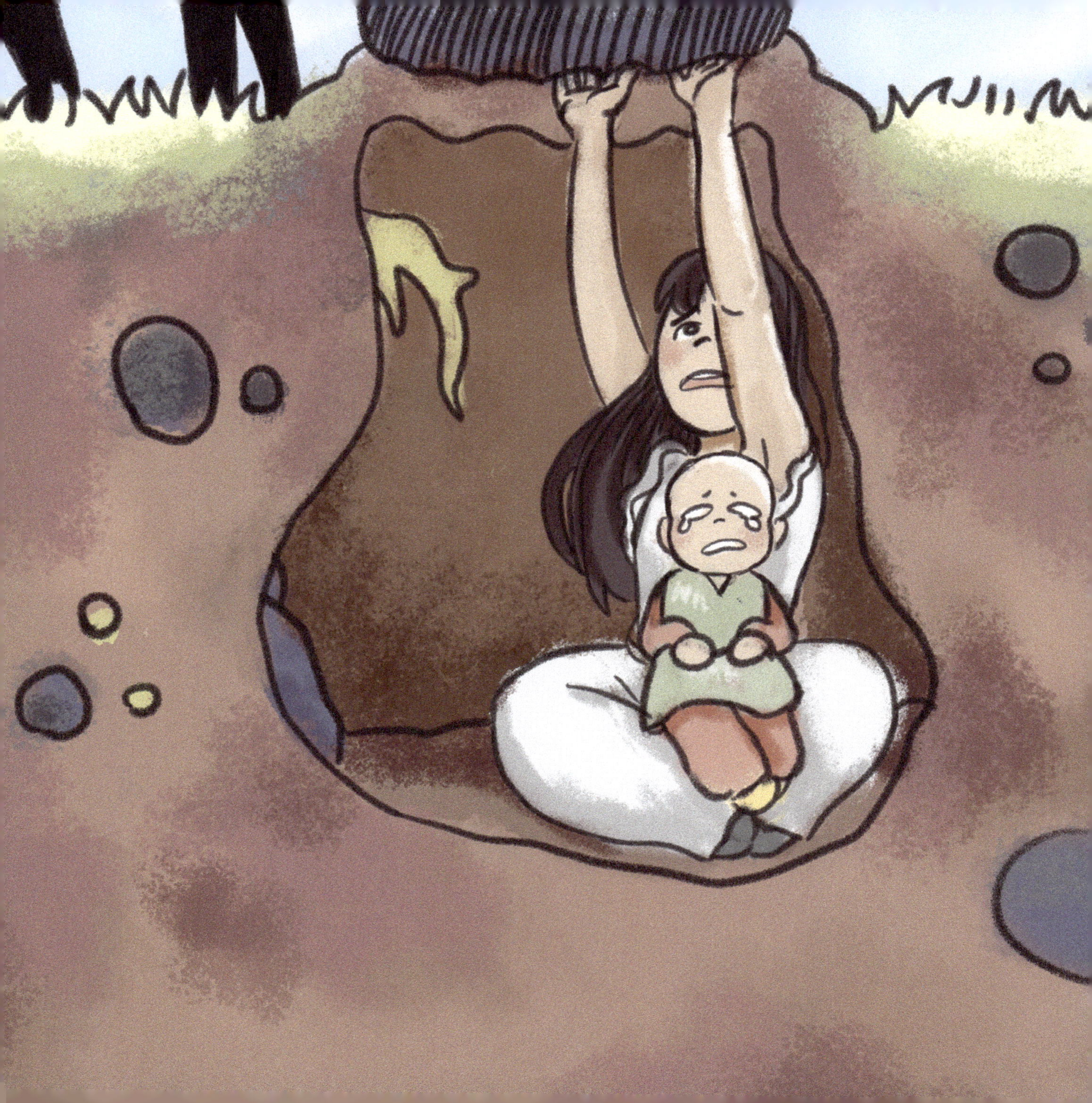

Hearing these words, the character with the high-pitched voice gathered all his courage and pushed the rock with his last two paws. He entered the molehill and saved the two sisters.

As the two sisters emerged from the shadow of the molehill, they saw that the face of the mysterious figure with the high-pitched voice was covered with dirt and scars. It was a wolf whose piercing eyes showed great vulnerability.

Grace burst out laughing. She laughed and giggled to the point of making the forest shake of curiosity. The animals came closer and began to laugh along with her.

Maya said:

-What is your name?

-My name is Eze. I have been living in this forest for many years, my paws were stolen by a villager from Mount Mouchi. Since then, I have been hiding in this part of the Sira forest, I miss my paws.

-But you have others at least. I don't even have a hair. No, I don't have hair. There is no hair. I don't have any hair. Maya, Grace has no hair.

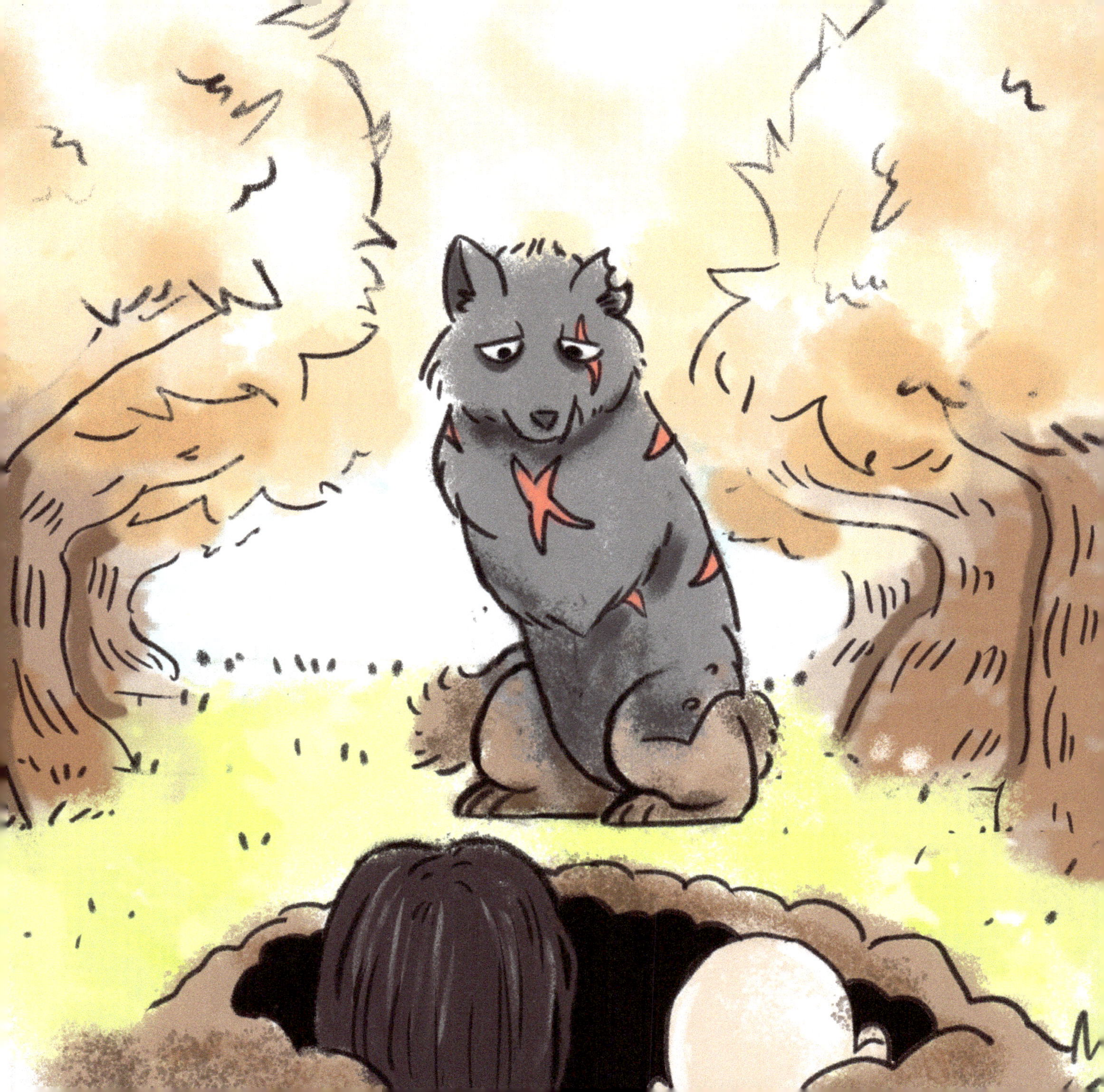

Maya looked at Grace and asked the wolf to share his story with her:

-Can you tell us what happened?

-I was walking through the forest with my pack when I heard a noise. The pack chose to ignore the noise, but I had a strange feeling that something was going to happen. And I was not wrong, burning arrows were thrown in our direction. The pack took fright and tried to avoid the arrows, while retaliating and trying to attack our assailant.

The situation got out of hand, I tried to stop them, but two arrows pierced my paws.

My pack fled, I had to relearn how to live with missing paws, learn to move and regain strength. I was not angry or fatalistic, I had to relearn how to live and rebuild myself.

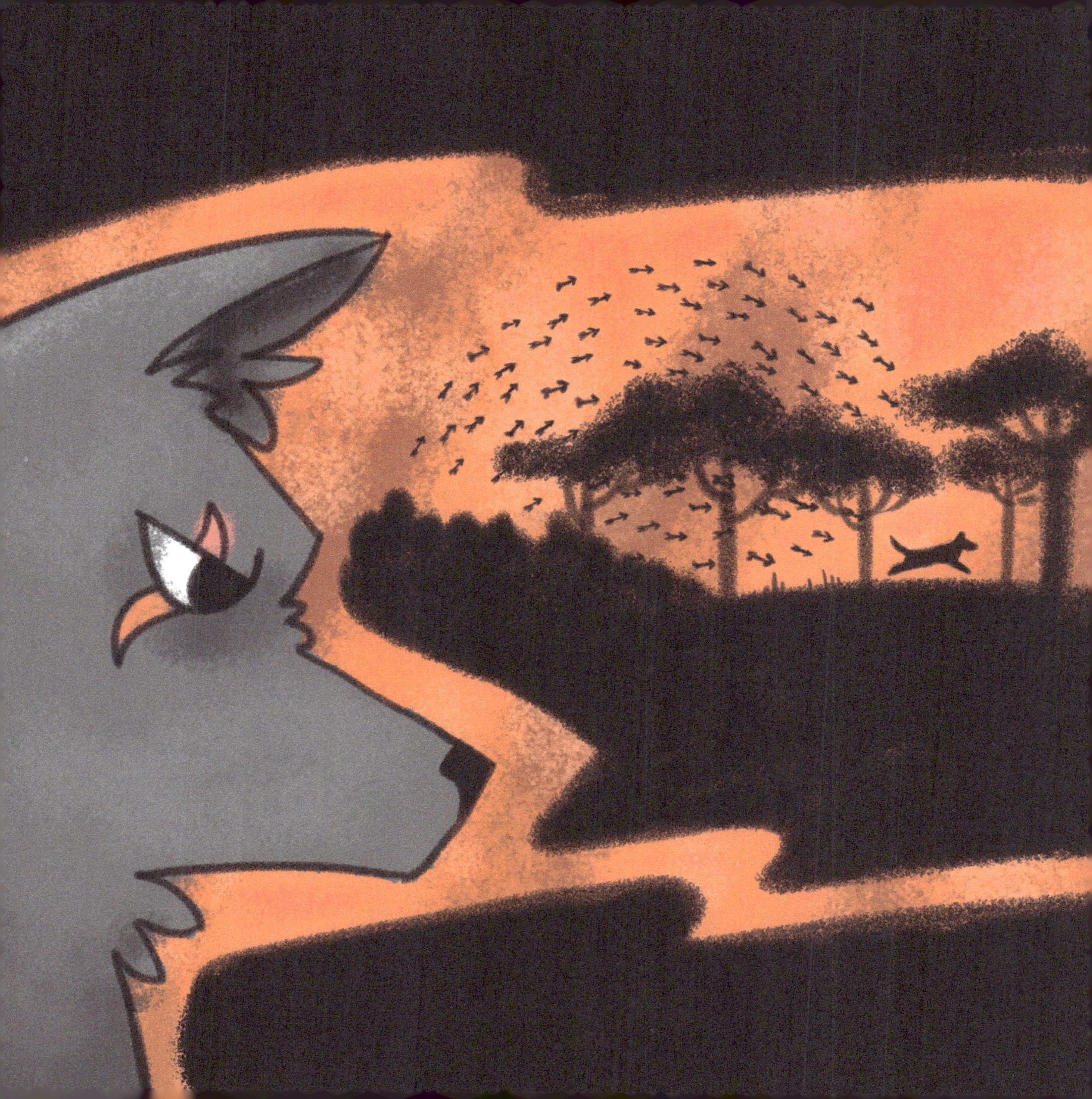

The animals had understood that this wolf had experienced rejection, humiliation, loneliness, violence, betrayal and disability.
Maybe that's why today he is who he is and that what could be terrible for some people, is part of life of his life.

"You know Mr. Wolf, I always thought you were too strong for a wolf. When you lost your paws, I thought that it had reduced your extraordinary capacity, but no. I feel that you have a new way of thinking. I even feel that you are even stronger," said a fox.

Maya placed her hand on her sister's heart and continued on her way, leaving the wolf behind.

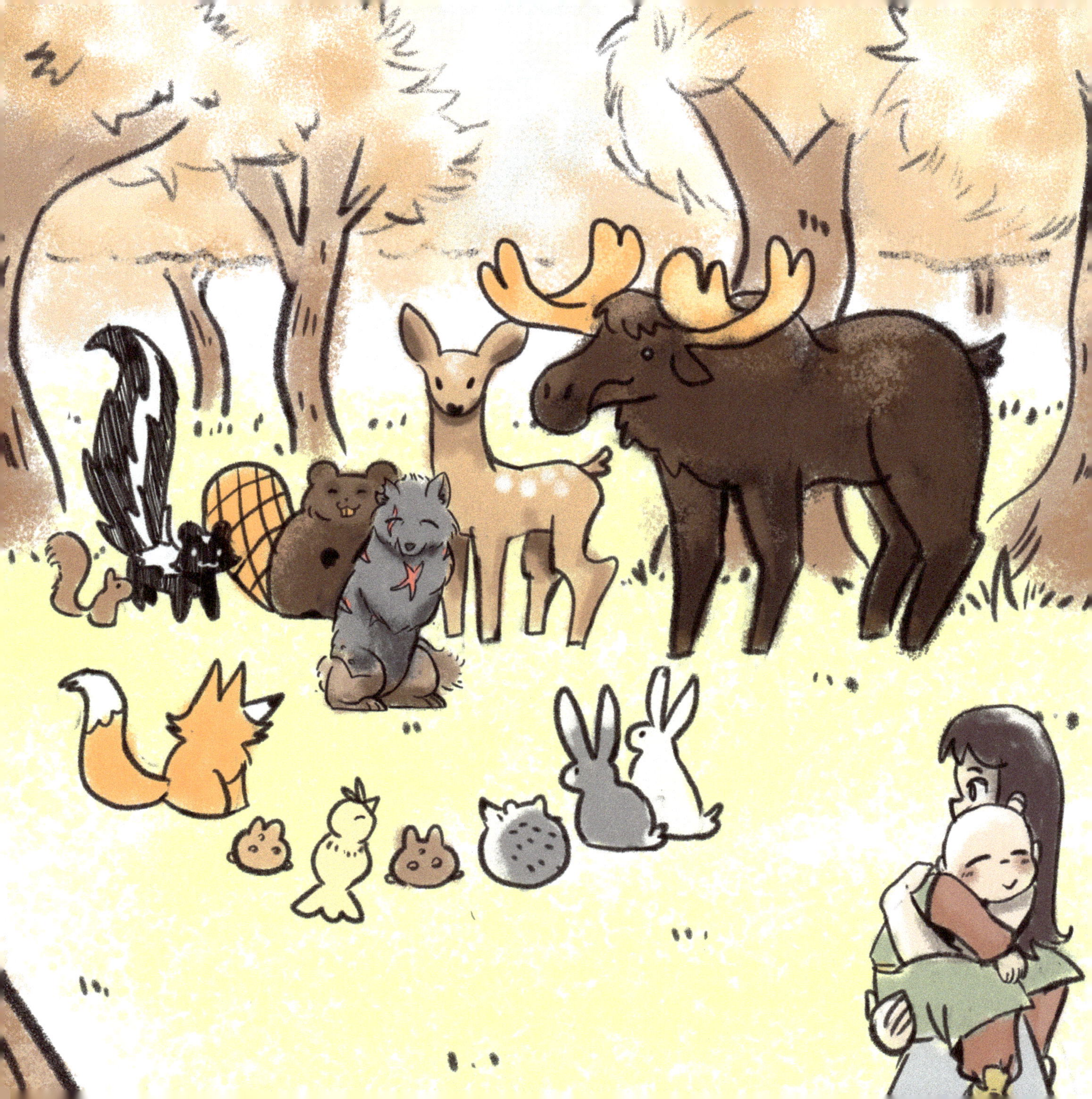

The two sisters went deeper into the forest, their bellies beginning to grumble. In the distance they saw an old stork near a fishy pond. The girls were surprised that the stork was not fishing. It was chatting with the fish, and seemed to be telling them its story. The two sisters came closer to listen to what the stork was saying to the fish. The stork looked hungry and weak, she sat down slowly, she looked sad.

Maya observed her and seeing her in this state of sadness and gloom, approached her and asked:

-O stork, why are you so sad and depressed?

-How can I not be sad, said the stork, I managed to live without fishing, the storks of the South and the East fed me, respected me. I am a stork who lived between the city of Kech and the province of Ace. I had a big and loving family… At least, I thought that they loved me for my generosity, my love and especially my fidelity. I was mistaken, I was naive. Yes, I was naïve…

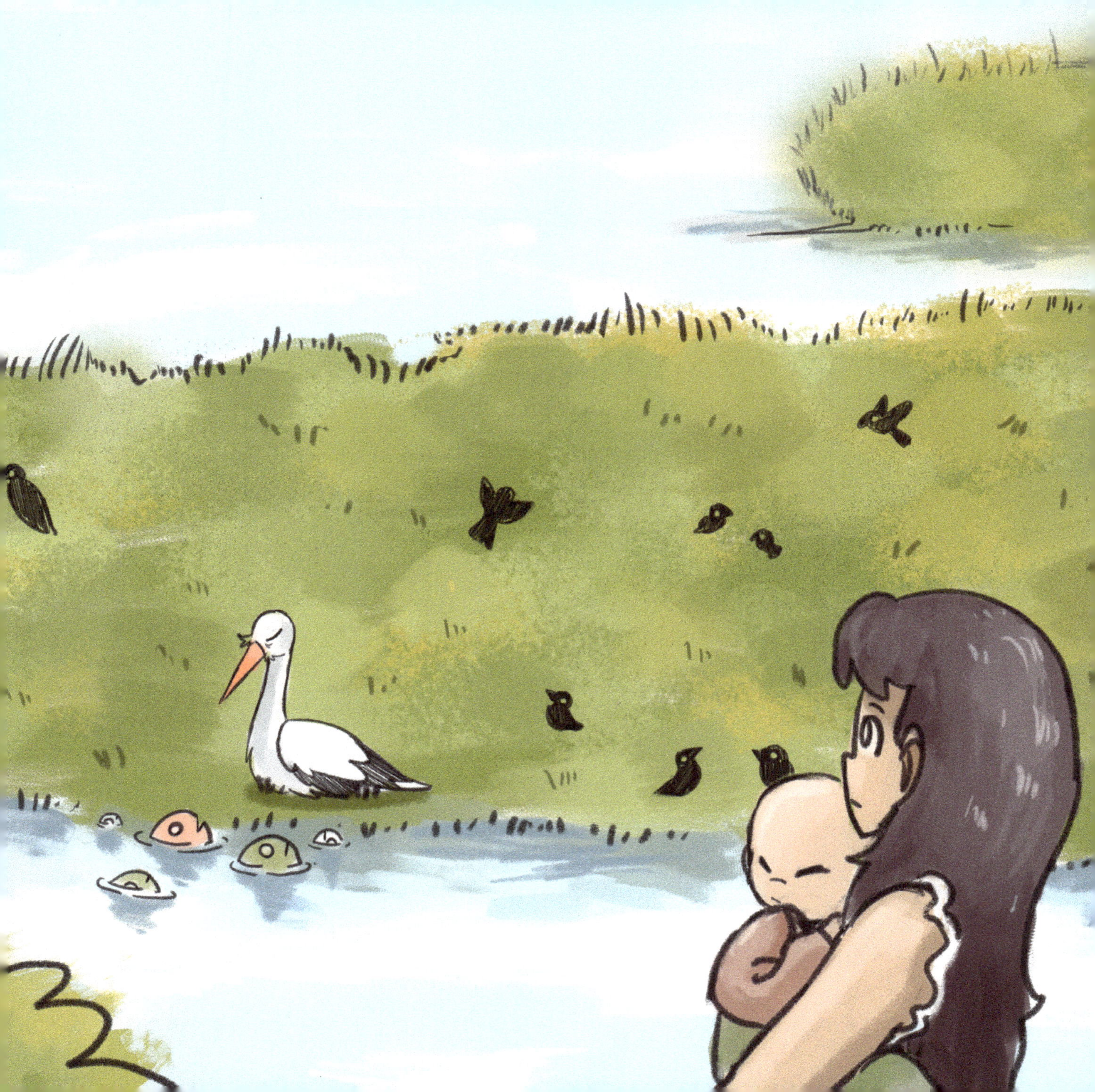

-Why do you say that? interrupted Grace.

-I was married more than 60 years to the King of the Storks, he was from Anca. When we got married, he chose to follow me to the province of Ace. Everyone knew him and respected him for his great generosity. He owned more than seven ponds filled with fish and no one was allowed to access them except him and his family. We had children; the first, Lah died for love. The second, Zia… I would have liked to tell you that she is dead, but no she is alive and well. The third, Dia as shy as a silent stream and comes to feed me every morning.

When my old husband died, Zia had conceived an army to steal the inheritance of the king of storks, namely the ponds and our house in Kech and Ace. Zia came to my house in Ace and cried and told me that she thought that my family would steal my property when her father died and that she did not want that. So, I asked her for advice, she told me that I had to fly to Kech to hide and that she would take care of everything.

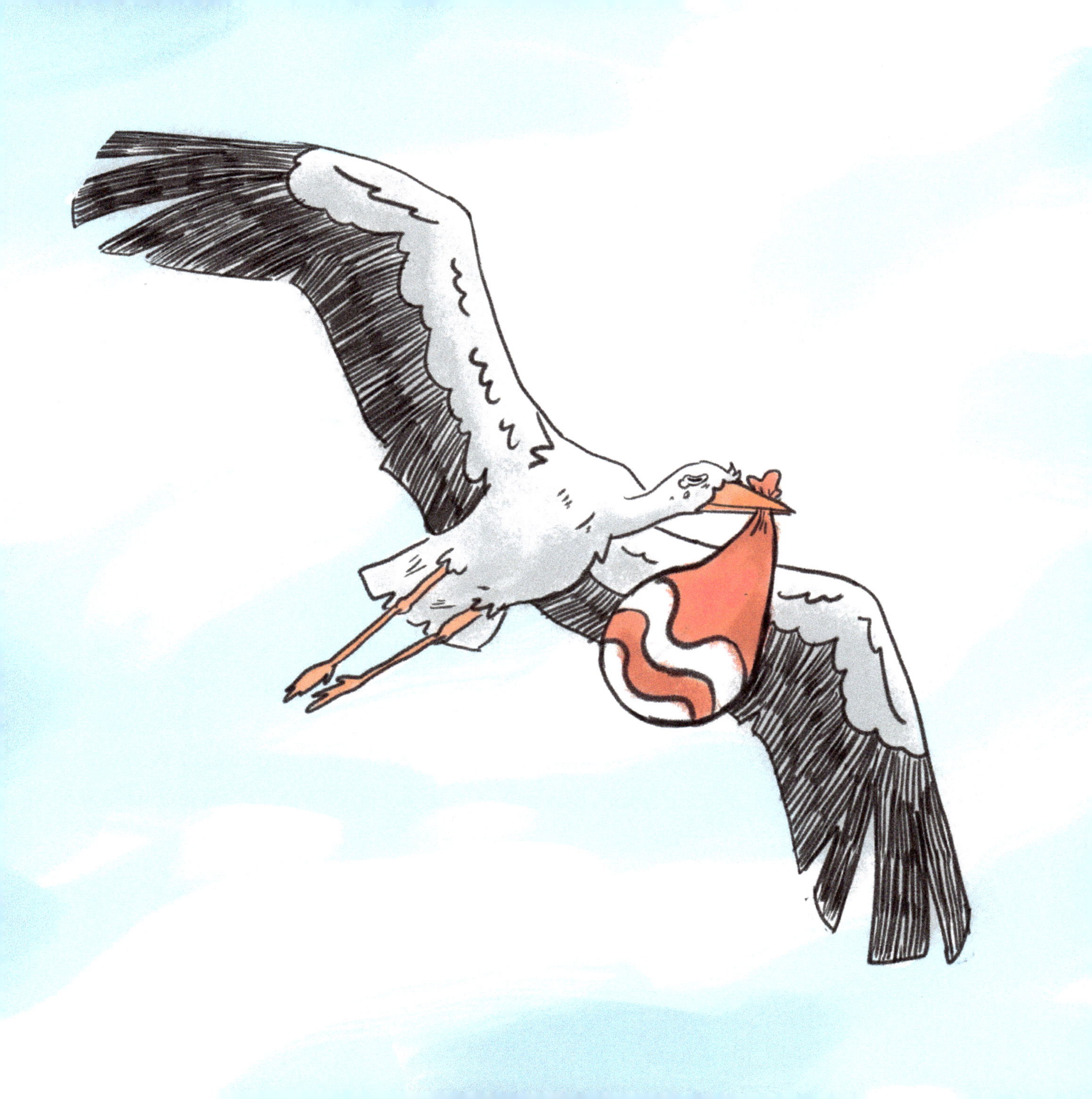

Dia saw me and stopped me, she told me not to move. She found this story rather suspicious, she asked me to trust her and to go and take refuge in her house. I did not understand, I was stubborn and I insisted to fly to Kech, for the love of her children, she asked me to listen to her and if I wanted to leave, I could leave the next day. I listened to her and then it was an opportunity for me to share a loving moment with my grandchildren. Dia flew over the hill where her mother lived and saw Zia selling her mother's things. The young stork looked over and saw a large pile of stuff and fish bones. She realized that Zia was stealing from her mother, so she went down to confront the greedy Zia. She thought; *If my sister turns into an enemy out of greed, I must fight, defend myself even if I lose the fight, I must not give up. I must save the honor of my family and our life by fighting.*

The two sisters fought; Dia crawled home with one leg missing. The only thing she said was that she had lost the fight and that it was my fault, that I had to stop believing Zia more than her. She cried and shared her pain. She cried that this had to stop and that I had to believe her. That she didn't care about our possessions, that she didn't care about our wealth because her greatest wealth was her children. From that day on, she never spoke of what had happened. She thought she had lost the battle.

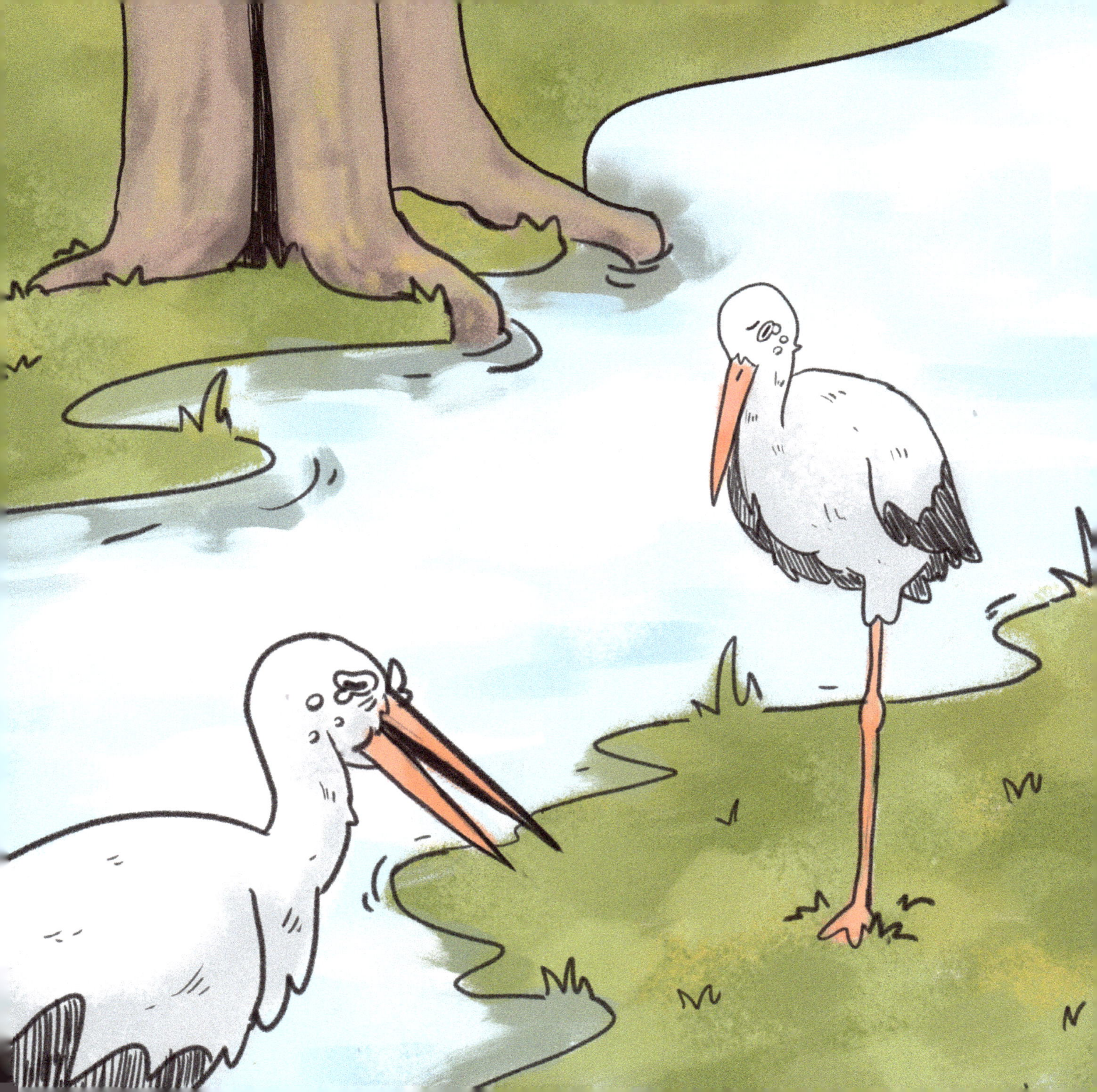

Zia banished me from my own homes and sold them to other storks. No storks dare to look me in the eyes, I lost the respect I was given. I wonder if they were respecting me because my husband was powerful or because I deserved that respect.

A few tears started to flow down Maya's face. She said to stork:

"Dia never lost the fight, on the contrary, she won it because she understood that her greatest wealth is her family. O stork, your wealth has never been your possessions, your wealth is your daughter, your grandchildren who until today have remained close to you. Love them, don't think about the past, live your present, you are not the one who is dead. Zia will understand later and way too late that greed is a sin, that the other storks do not respect her but fear her, but until when? Until another stork does exactly the same thing."

The stork was moved and kissed Maya on the head and said:

"Thank you, my daughter, I see that you are as brave as Dia. I offer you my last bracelet, keep it as a souvenir of an old stork."

Grace took her sister by the hand and asked her if they could go on. Maya took Grace in her arms, waved to the stork and continued on her way.

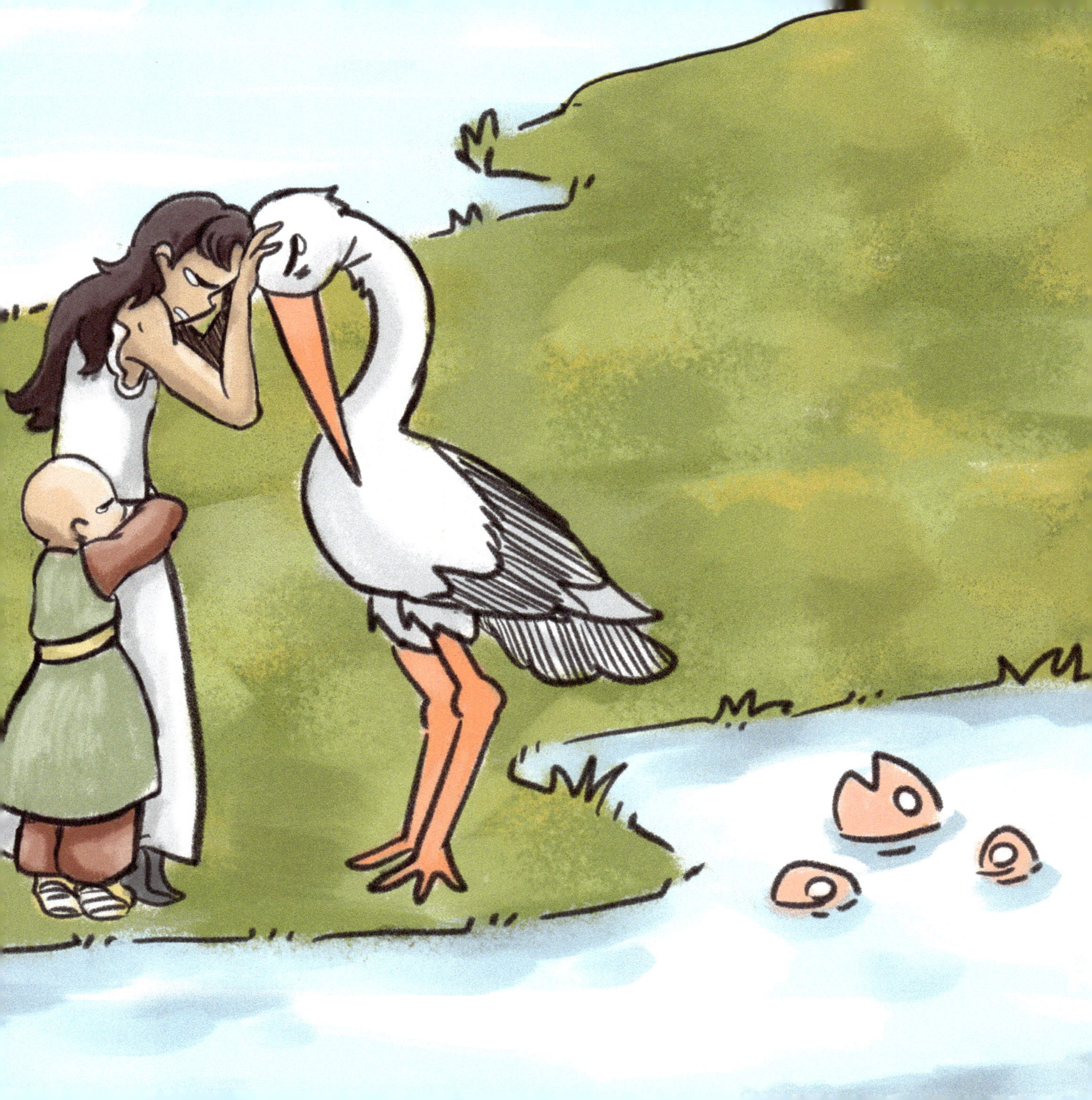

The sisters arrived in another village: the village of fire. A very poor village facing the water village.

Maya had read about this village, and decided to tell her sister the story:

"It is said that the fire king allied himself with the greatest sorcerer on the continent to try to steal the wealth of the water village. The sorcerer turned him into a waterman and was able to enter the village and see if the water people were as rich as they said. He spent a few days there and observed the life of the water people, he saw no great difference between them. He asked for an audience with the water king, he had so many questions to ask him. He went to court and was received by the water king. He asked him what made them different from the other peoples, like the one of fire.

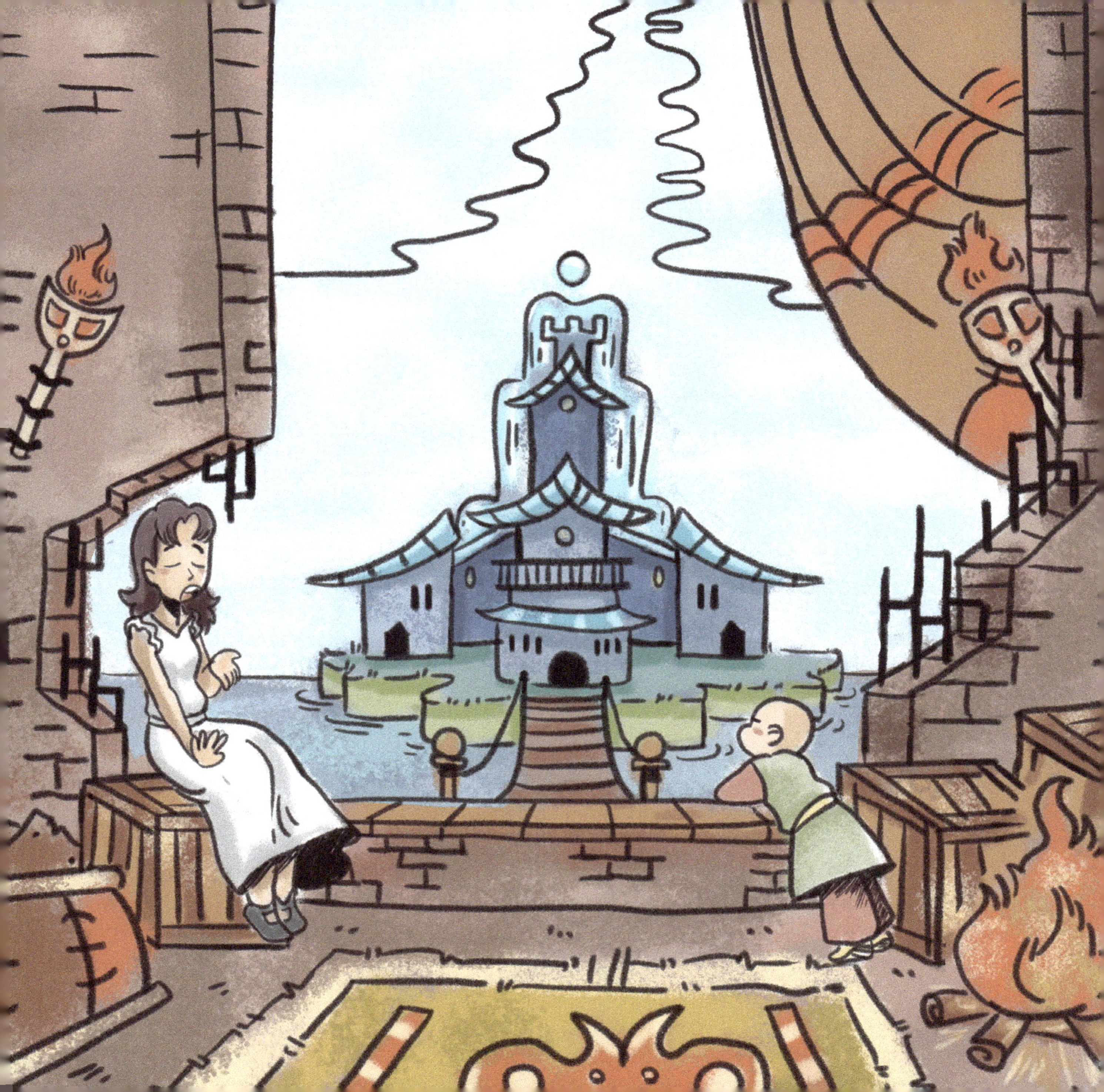

Surprised by this question the king smiled and answered:

-Water corresponds to a variable temperament, which can be as angry as calm. This element is opposed to fire, but they are the most powerful elements. What are they without the earth and what could the earth be without them? What are we without fire and what is fire without us?

-You know, said the fire, I have learned something from all this, your wealth is not what you have more than us, but it is part of your wisdom.

The fire revealed its identity and added:

-We don't need to fight about who is more important or richer, because we are all important. We complement each other, you are not richer than us and we are not richer than you."

Grace looked at Maya and continued to walk further into the fire village.

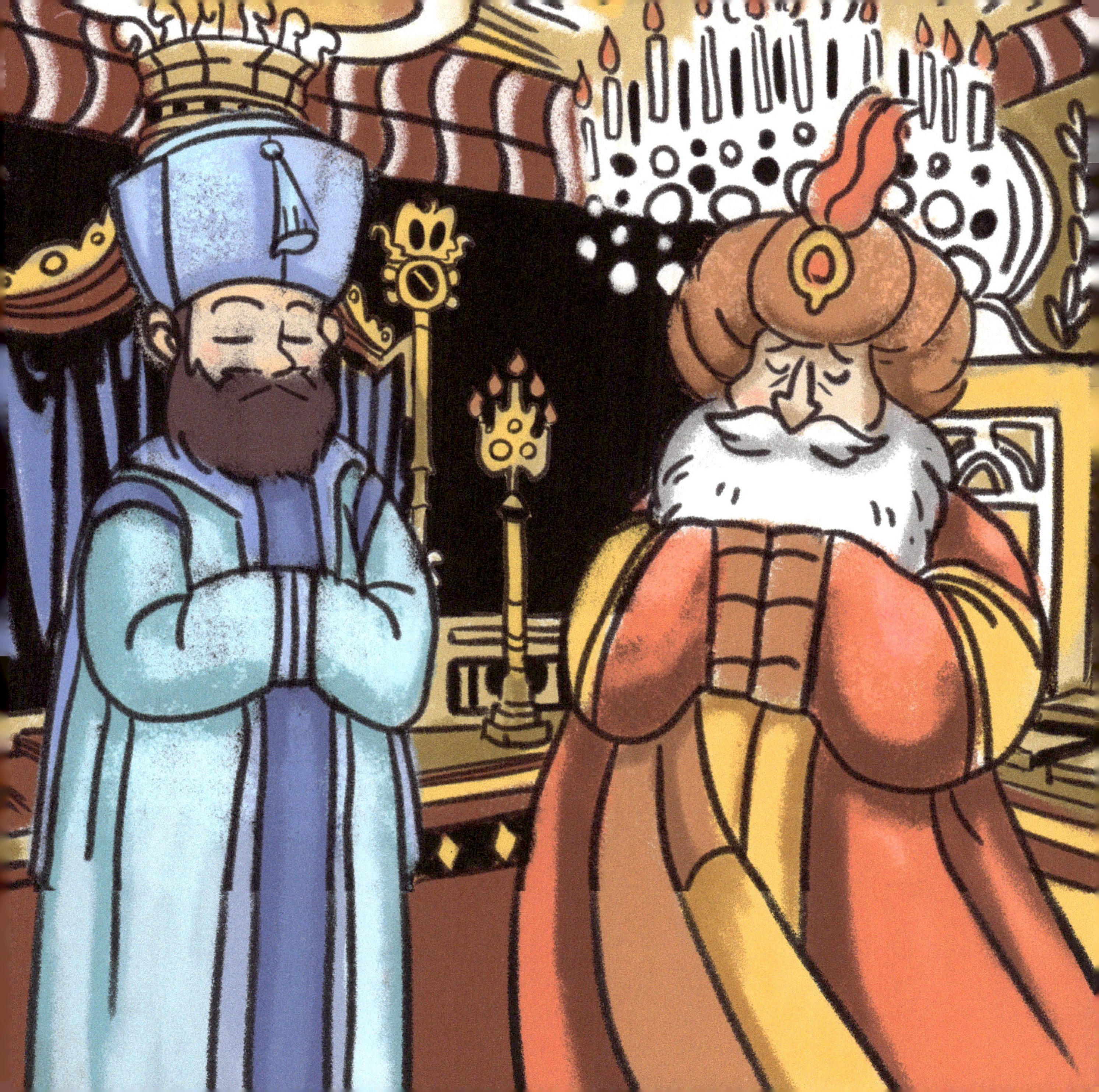

They arrived near the old Port de Bourg. They met dozens of young seagulls. They were gossiping and commenting on the clothes, manners, and personalities of passers-by. Maya listened to them and her stomach tightened with each mockery of the seagulls. She didn't understand how these young seagulls could be so judgmental. It didn't make sense to her.

She continued to watch them and the leader of the seagulls spotted her, she walked up to her and said:

-And you, what are you looking at?

-Nothing, I let my thoughts fly.

-Who allowed you to look at us? In the Port of Bourg, we are the ones making the law.

-I don't want any problems; we can stop our conversation now.

-Leave her alone, Stelle! said another seagull called Bia.

-Don't interfere, Bia.

-Yes, I do want to meddle, this poor girl makes me sad. She looks lost and helpless.

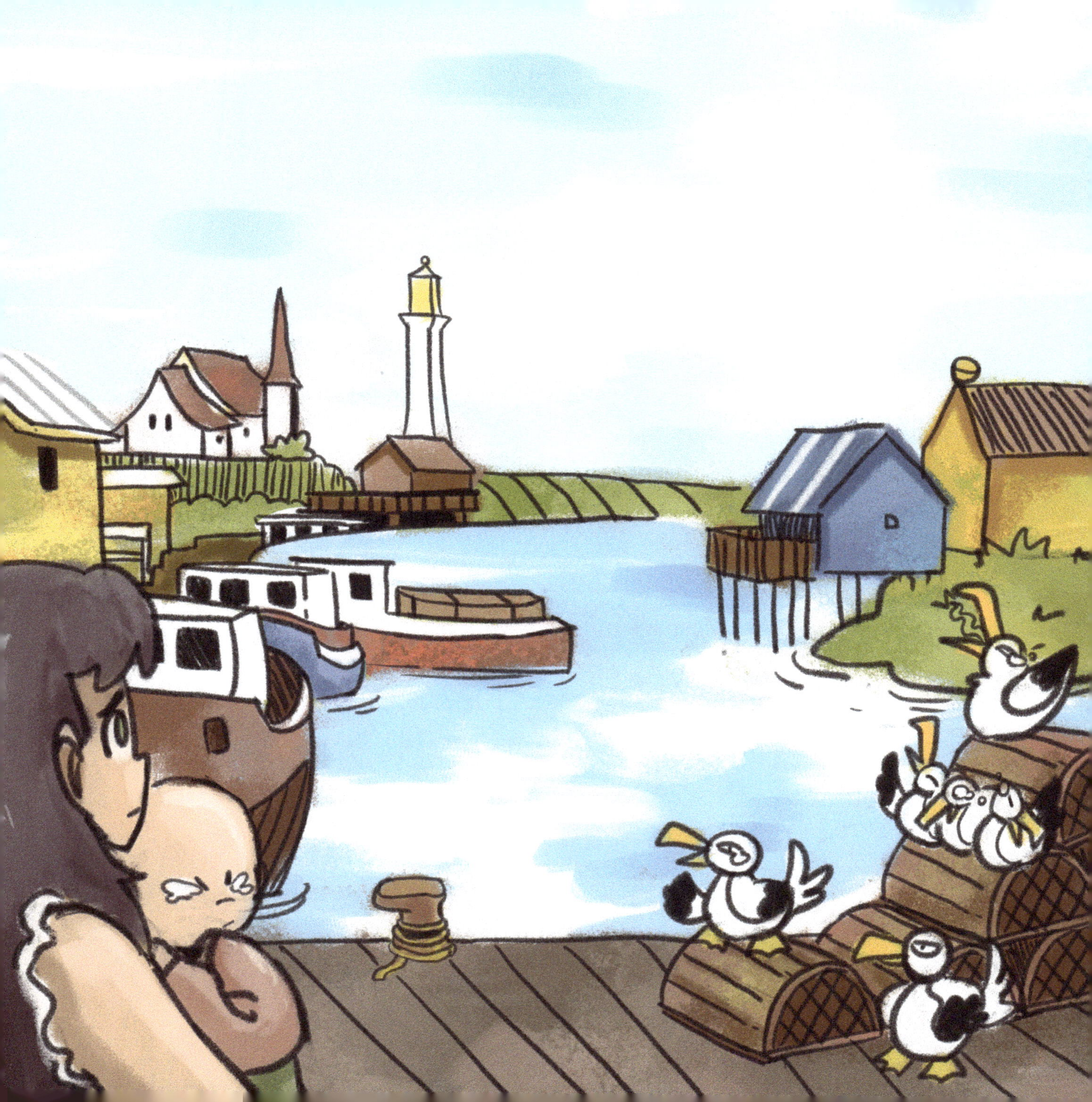

The weeks passed and the sisters developed a beautiful friendship with Bia. She helped them find food and shelter. She introduced them to a sailor named Oger so that the girls could plan their sea voyages.

The two sisters loved spending time with Oger; they had much in common and learned a lot from him. Maya felt a wave of energy around him. He was attentive and gave Maya life advice that she never had.

This seemed to displease Bia who began to develop a great deal of jealousy towards Maya. She decided to move away from the two sisters, not see them anymore and to avoid them.

Maya felt betrayed and did not understand why Bia was acting this way. Bia didn't want to talk, when she came across the sisters at the Port even a hello was difficult to offer. She developed a wave of hatred that turned the color of her wings to black.

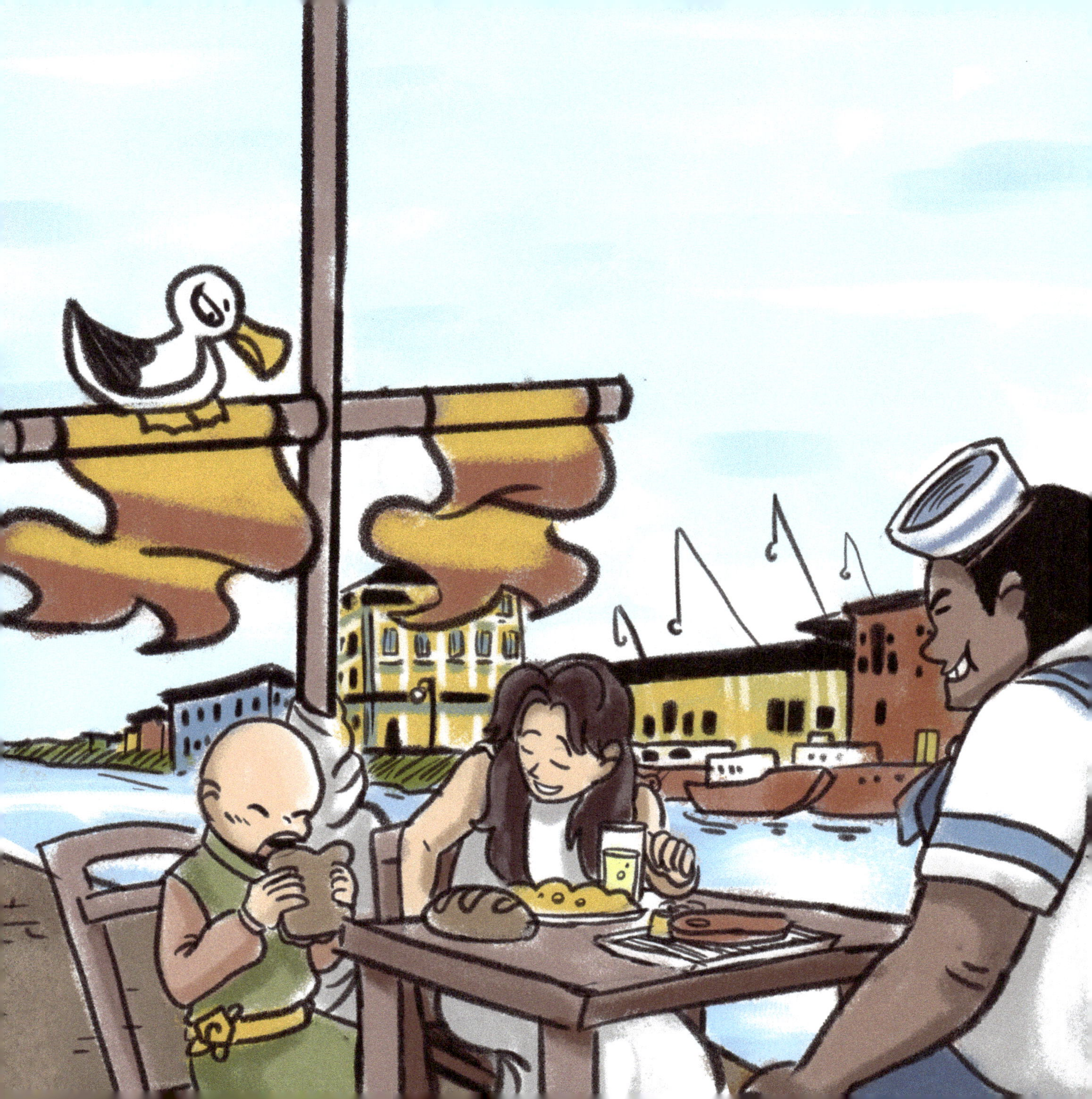

Maya wanted to understand Bia's behavior and why she changed overnight.

Maya went alone to meet Bia. The seagull told her:

"I don't think you are a fair person; you only think about yourself and you use your sister and your beauty to get your way."

Speechless, Maya started to cry, Bia's words had hurt her deeply.

With a flick of her wings Bia flew away.

Maya went home in tears and decided not to share what had happened with Grace, but Grace didn't need a thousand words to understand that her sister was sad.

Days passed and Grace wanted to follow the road to the sun to find her parents.

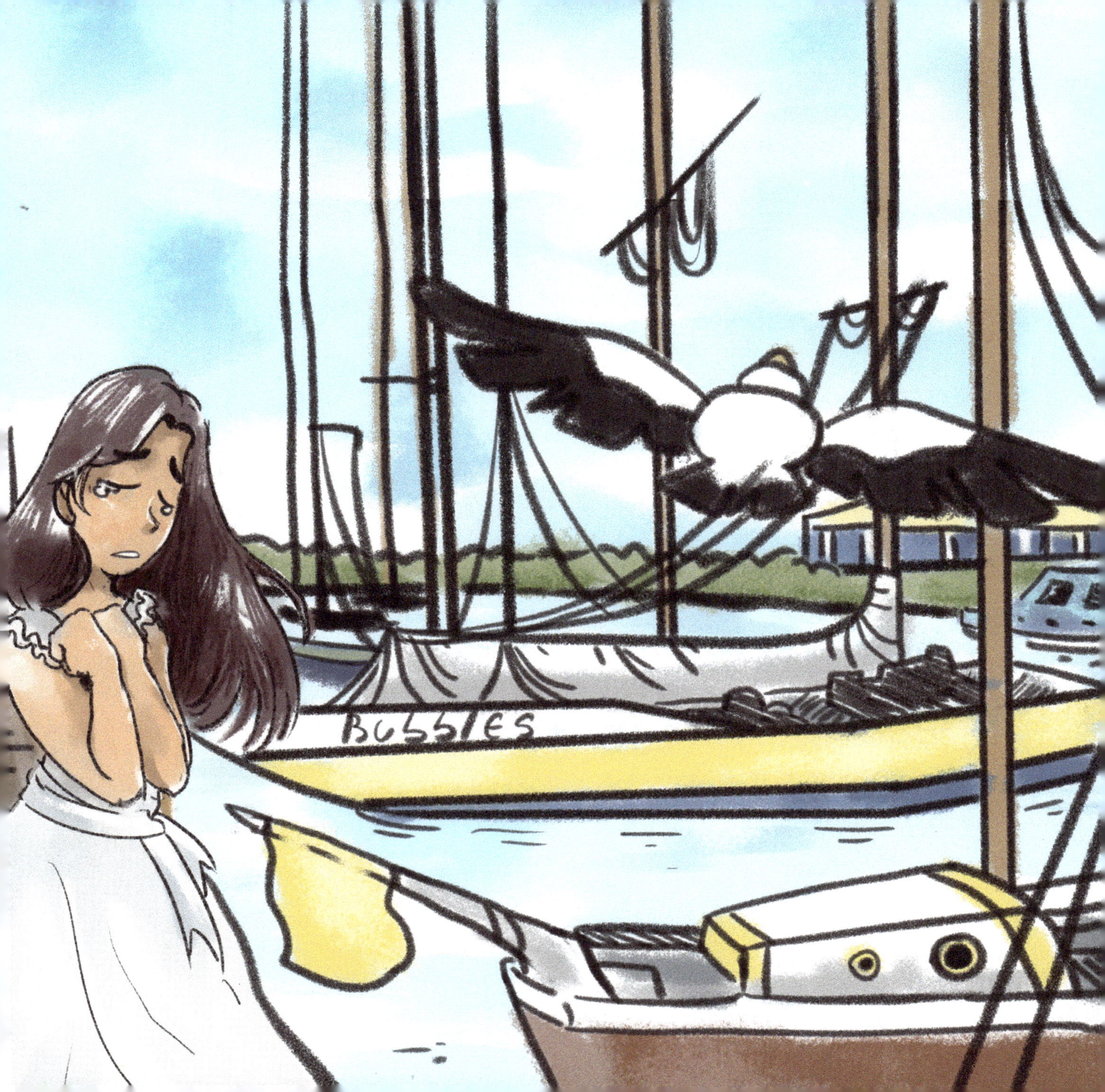
BUBBLES

A sea voyage was necessary. She went to Oger for advice, and he helped her organize part of the trip. She hugged him to thank him. Bia passed by at the same time with her gull gang and ordered the gulls to attack Maya. Bia changed her color; her body became completely black.

The seagulls flew away at full speed and tried to attack Maya.
When she screamed with all her strength:
-Enough! You are angry with me because you find me different and do not appreciate the fact that people can be deeply kind without expecting or asking for anything in return. You don't accept that people have a thirst for knowledge. You spend your days talking about strangers, denouncing, criticizing.

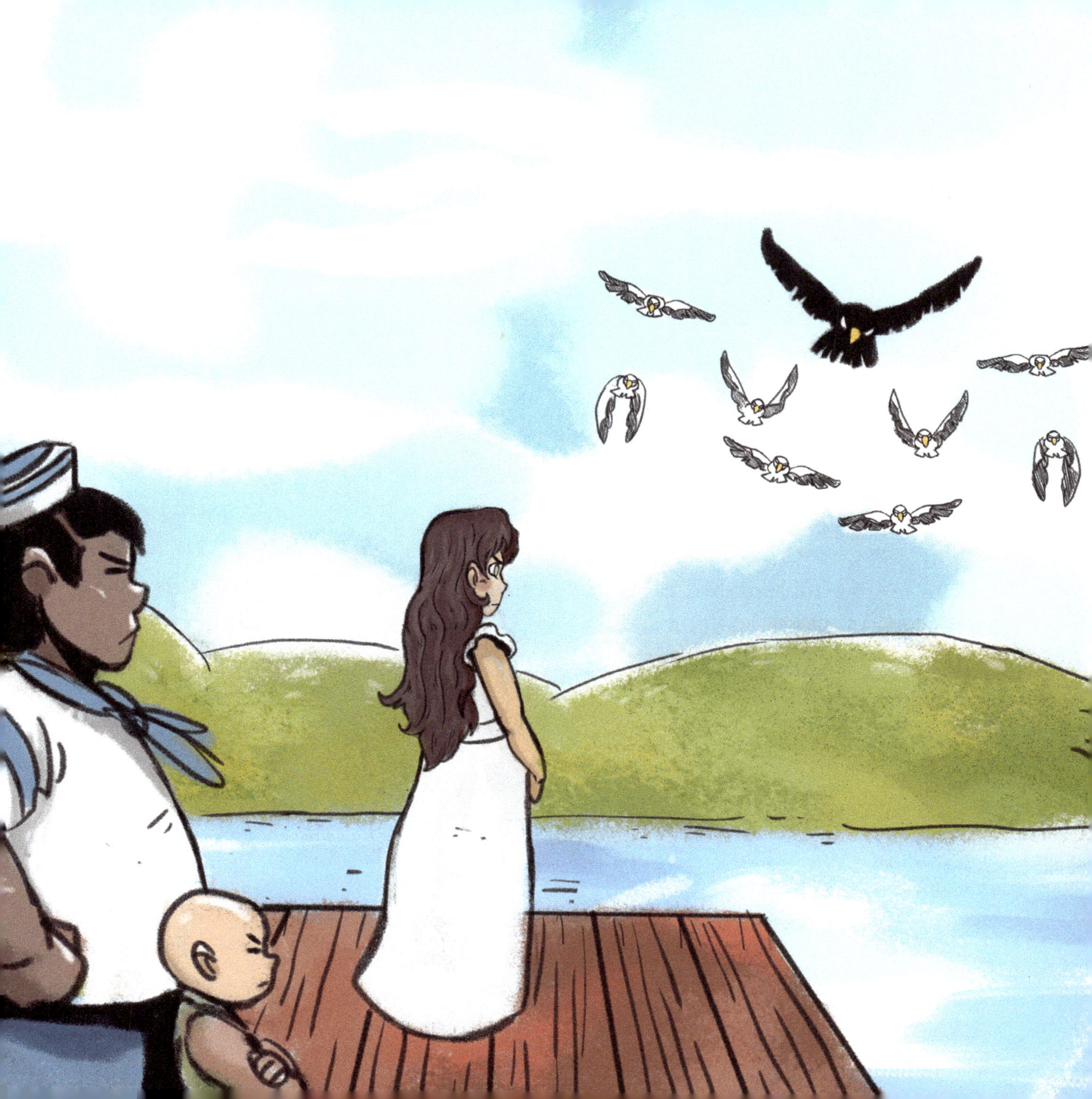

I was too proud to cry, too thoughtful to speak and it was at my expense. I don't have to suffer because of you, you don't want me in your life. So, I accept it, I'm glad that I met you and made good memories with you. I will not forget them, never. I will keep in memory every happy moment, but I will remember your last acts. They will give me strength and will.
I will continue to meet seagulls like you, but like today, I will move on and leave you behind. I wish you to have a happy life but I don't wish that it will be with me. Goodbye.
Maya took her sister and walked towards a ship.

The sisters continued their adventures and never ceased to marvel at the ambivalence of the world.

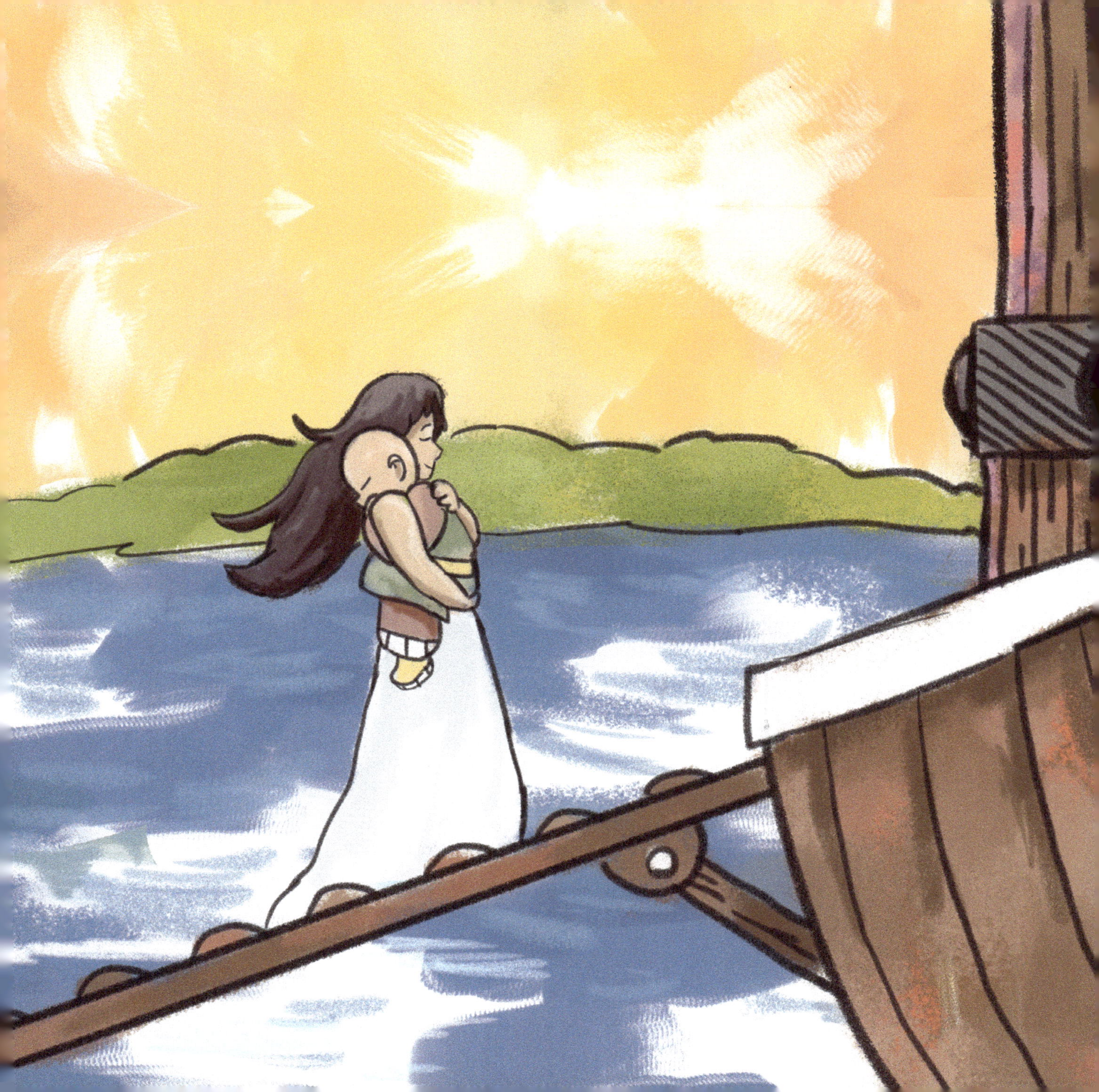

THE END

CPSIA information can be obtained
at www.ICGtesting.com
Printed in the USA
BVHW011447050223
657830BV00015B/686

9 789948 808619